NINE LIVES

HELEN JULIET

CW00551895

Nine Lives
Copyright © 2022 by Helen Juliet

1

___

CHARLIE

I HAD PRETTY LOW EXPECTATIONS FOR MY TWENTY-FIRST birthday. But even I didn't think I'd get evicted *and* robbed blind all in one afternoon.

Happy fucking birthday to me.

In retrospect, I shouldn't have been surprised. My stepfather's hated me since the moment he walked into my mum's life, even more so after she passed last year. But I really thought my inheritance was safe.

Shows what I know.

"Gio, please," I beg down the phone. Standing in the rain on my own front doorstop is a pitiful enough look anyway. But there's a very real danger I'm going to start crying as well. I refuse to give him that satisfaction, though, so I bite the inside of my cheek and screw my eyes shut for a second. "Be reasonable."

He scoffs on the other end of the call. "Oh, I've *been* reasonable," he tells me.

I think he's driving his van between jobs from the traffic sounds I can hear. At least I should be grateful that he isn't off his face down the pub. Not that I'm especially hopeful of a good outcome either way.

He's changed the locks, and when I checked my bank balance just now, it's at zero. My regular account and my savings, where I had my inheritance from Mum. All gone. I'd had a horrible suspicion before that he might somehow have had access to my login. Now I guess I know for sure.

"I've put up with you for years," he continues to drawl down the phone at me, almost like he's bored. "Your mum's bitch lawyer was very clear. I had to put a roof over your head until you turned twenty-one. Done."

I shake my head. "So I'll move out," I cry.

I was planning on that anyway with my savings. Taking care of Mum as the cancer slowly took her from me was a full-time job—god knows one Gio wasn't going to do—and after she was gone, it took me several months to haul myself out of the depression that followed. I had to, though, when Gio started demanding rent. So I got part-time hours at a shop in town to appease him.

I'd been relying on the inheritance for a deposit to rent my own place, however. Just a room in a house share, but somewhere that was all mine. That was finally going to be my escape. I've even been looking at places this week in anticipation of the funds finally being unlocked. I was dreaming of that freedom being the only birthday present I was going to get.

I guess I've still got a version of freedom. He's made it very clear he's kicking me out of his life.

"I need my inheritance, though," I plead with him. "That was mine from Mum. Please, if you give it back, you'll never have to hear from me again."

He laughs, a nasty sound that sends a cold shiver down my spine. "Oh, you're right there, mate. I *won't* ever hear from you again. I'm done. That money is my back payment for having to put up with a little fucking pussy like you. I'm *owed* that money."

I take a shaky breath, my heart pounding in my chest with real fear. He's actually doing this to me. It's really happening.

"Gio, please. I'll leave tonight. I'll clear out my stuff, and you'll never hear from me again, just like you said. I just need some of that money to get on my feet."

There's a chilling pause. "I've already got rid of you. What's all this bleating about? You always were such a soft fucking poofter. I'm hanging up and blocking your number. Don't even *think* about being at the house when I get back. Now piss the fuck off."

The call goes dead.

I stare at the screen as rain falls on it. I should probably be more worried about water getting into the circuitry, but I'm so numb with shock I'm not thinking straight.

I have nothing.

No clothes other than the soaking ones on my back. No cash unless you count the couple of quid in my wallet. About a fiver on my Oyster card that will do me two journeys, max.

I can't breathe.

Options, *options*. Work. I'm not due to get paid for another couple of weeks, and even then, it'll only be a couple of hundred quid, but it's better than nothing. *Way* better. I fumble with shaking fingers to find the number and call. I can try and ask for an advance and also more hours. I'm still not sure what I'm going to do tonight, but it's still only the afternoon and it's summer. I've got hours until it'll get dark. There's still time to sort…something.

"Hello?" a distracted voice answers the phone at the crappy clothes shop where I've been working for the past few months. It's all badly made and cheap as chips, but at least I think it's ethical and not stitched by kids in some far-off country. I don't recognise the guy, but that's not surprising. Everyone there seems to be in various zombified states. It's not exactly a raucous social circle.

"Hi! Hello!" I squeak, trying not to sound hysterical but probably failing. "Is Jesse there today? I really need to speak to him." He's my manager, and I'm hoping he'll know what to do—or if anything *can* be done.

"Uhh…no. I don't think so," the guy says sounding extremely disinterested.

I bite my tongue and force myself not to lose my shit. "Could you possibly find out?" I ask as patiently as I can. "It's an emergency. Oh—this is Charlie Scarpa, by the way."

The guy sighs like I'm being totally unreasonable. He doesn't say anything. He just puts me on hold. So I wait.

And wait.

In the rain.

Then the line eventually goes dead after about ten minutes.

I'm feeling really bloody sick now.

I genuinely don't want to be hanging around when Gio comes back to the house—my house which I've lived in *my whole life*—so I wander in the rain down to the nearest bus stop that at least has a cover over it.

The line is just an engaged tone now. I try a couple more times, but then I realise it's gone five o'clock and the shop will be closed now. I'm guessing the guy left the damn receiver off the hook, and no calls will get through until someone notices, most likely in the morning.

"Fuck!" I yell over the noise of the traffic, startling a couple of nearby pigeons. I chew on my thumbnail as my vision starts narrowing down into a darkened tunnel of complete and utter panic.

I really, *really* don't want to sleep outside tonight. Not on a bench or a doorstep or down some dodgy alley that stinks of piss. I guess I could try and find a homeless shelter—I'm *homeless, fuck*—but that would require a lot of searching on the internet. My phone battery is dwindling, and I don't have my charger on me. Why would I? It's in my bedroom, along with all my clothes and my other worldly possessions. I think of the teddy Mum gave me when I was little—the one I used to cling to when it became clear her chemo wasn't working—and choke down a sob.

I'd really love to cuddle Teddy right about now, but I can't curl up and admit defeat. I'm an adult, and I have to take care of myself.

I've spent my life in such a narrow bubble, though. Mum and I looked after each other. Gio bullied us both. I was never sure why she married him. I guess she was just afraid of being alone. Since school, I've lost touch with any friends I might have had. My whole world was reduced down to her appointments and care, which I was absolutely happy to do. But it's left me pretty inexperienced for a twenty-one-year-old.

My breath catches, and I gasp, feeling the rain on my tongue as a wave of dizziness washes through me. I'm so alone and can't think of a single person to turn to for help. Not a friend or a teacher. I could go to the police but say what? If Gio had access to my account, that means what he's done is probably technically legal. Nothing in my life so far has prepared me for being so totally fucked.

But then it's like I snap back to life, a very clear idea forming in my mind.

I *am* inexperienced. I might be metaphorically fucked, but in real life…

Never.

People pay money for that kind of thing, don't they? Big money.

I rub my chest. Am I delusional? No. But I sure am desperate.

It's not like I've been guarding my virginity like a dragon with its hoard of treasure. I've just been all-consumed with Mum's health. I worked out I was gay back in my early teens. Obviously, she was fine with it, but I knew Gio would hate me even more if I officially came out. Not that he held back from speculating. But all in all, dating and sex didn't seem all that important.

Until now.

My body is the only thing I have left to sell. If it means cash in hand and a warm bed for the night, I'll take it. But… how? God, I'm so bloody naive. All I can think is to head to Soho. But it's not like prostitutes hang around on street corners. I'd have to find somewhere, if there even is anywhere like that in London. It would be pretty underground if there was anything.

I consider my phone. I could sign up to that app—the one where people subscribe to see your naughty videos. But I doubt my battery would last long enough to set anything up, let alone film something. And where would I film? I have no privacy. A public toilet? That sounds even worse than sleeping rough.

So I come back around to Soho, the queerest part of London. There's a bus that goes from this very stop to there, so I'd have enough on my Oyster to get there and then maybe somewhere else for the night.

Fuck me. Anxiety is churning like curdled yoghurt in my stomach. I don't think I'm particularly special to look at, although I've been called cute a lot. But guys are kinky, right? Someone's *got* to get off on the idea of popping my cherry.

I feel a pang in my chest, but fuck it. I can't be precious about anything stupid like love or romance. This is the world's oldest profession for a reason. Virginity is a social construct anyway, right? All I'll need to do is lie back and think of England.

And do my best not to cry.

No. I'll lie back and think of being *warm* and *dry* for the night.

As if the universe is trying to stop me from talking myself out of this crazy plan, the bus I need appears in the distance.

Fine. I'll head to Soho and then work out where to go. Maybe one of those shops that sell the toys and leather gear and stuff. Or one of the clubs. Not the shiny bars that play happy pop and dance songs. One of the darker, hidden ones.

Oh.

Oh, fuck.

The breath I take properly expands my chest for the first time since I realised my key no longer worked. It's not exactly relief, but like the beginnings of relief.

I know where to go.

2

MILLER

I ALWAYS SUSPECTED MY FATHER THOUGHT OF ME AS A JOKE. But as I look around the sum total of my inheritance, I think it was perhaps more sinister than that.

I think he might have actually hated me.

"I know it's not much," says the manager forlornly by my side. He's an older gent by the name of Paul. With a white head of hair and a neat white beard, he's dressed in jeans and a polo shirt that clings to his rounded belly, giving him a sort of casual Father Christmas kind of vibe.

Not really the guy I'd expected to be running a gay strip club.

It's a Friday evening, and the place is about half full of blokes in suits and sparkly twinks in not much at all. Most of the latter probably work here. I'm not sure yet. But I get the feeling that their flirting with the suits isn't entirely genuine. A slim but muscular guy spins lazily around one of the poles on the stage in nothing but a thong and thigh-high boots with six-inch heels. Some of the crowd are half-heartedly cheering him on, but nobody feels particularly interested in it all.

It's sad and seedy, rather like my old man was.

He married very late in life to a much younger woman. All due respect to my mum, I think she knew exactly what she was signing up for, which was to pop out an acceptable amount of heirs in exchange for a ridiculous amount of money. I'm glad she's outlived him, and I hope she'll be happy off in Spain now.

She was the only one who ever showed me any kindness growing up.

I always suspected that my father's 'teasing' over my being gay came from a darker place. I'm convinced now more than ever that he was gay and too ashamed to live an authentic life. I'd feel sorry for him if he hadn't been such a tyrannical bastard.

My older brothers are just like him in all their coldness and cruelty. Of course, Gilbert got the global multi-million silk industry, and Victor got the racing horses and stables, both of which have been in our family for generations.

And I get the dirty little secret that Father wanted no one to know about whilst he was still alive. My brothers had an absolute field day during the reading of the will. In fact, I'm sure they're going to be dining out on this humiliation for the rest of my life.

Which is why I fully intend on selling it as fast as possible. But one look at the finances tells me I'm going to need to untangle a whole bloody lot before that can happen. And I'm not going to bother with a fancy refurb if I'm just going to sell it off, but damn it, a tidy and a lick of paint is going to go a *long* way. Not to mention steaming the sticky carpets.

I look at Paul, however, and wonder what he sees. He appears embarrassed and downbeat, like he really cares about this dive and what I think of it. Curious.

"Do you want to see the private rooms?" he asks with an attempt at a smile. "I don't think any of them are in use yet."

I narrow my eyes at him. "In use for what?"

He shrugs. "We don't ask. Mr Soldi said cash in hand was fine to look the other way."

Holy fuck. It's worse than I thought. I've inherited a *brothel.*

"Nope. Nuh-uh. That stops now," I say firmly, raising a finger and my eyebrows as I meet his gaze. "If it's not being regulated, that's dangerous, not to mention illegal. Who's using them? Patrons?"

I know the answer from Paul's uncomfortable expression. "Yeah...usually with the boys." He squares his shoulders. "I look after them, though. Nobody does nothing they don't want to."

I growl, finding that unlikely. But I'm warmed by his fierce protectiveness over the dancers. Perhaps that's what he's seeing as he shows me around. Not the walls or the stage, but the guys who clock in every day to this dreary corner of Soho called Bootleg.

I rub my temples, trying to fend off the oncoming headache. My business degree did *not* prepare me for this, and it's nothing like the half a dozen companies I've bought out, fixed up, and sold on over the past several years.

Still, it's now my responsibility. I'm not going to let anyone down.

"Right," I say firmly, clapping my hands together. I have to shout over the music, but Paul seems to hear me well enough. "Here's what we're going to do. We'll see out the weekend, then go on hiatus for two weeks. That gives us a couple of days to get the word out that we're refurbishing. Everyone will get paid in full whilst I oversee cleaning and repairs, not to mention straightening up the books. *No* more cash in hand for fucking in the back rooms. No more illegal *anything* now it's my name on the line."

Paul nods and looks around in the darkness. "Okay, boss.

It'll be nice to clean up a little, I must admit." He seems happy enough.

The lad on the pole has finished his routine, so the music has quietened a bit, and it's just the swirling blue lights illuminating the room. The men are drinking and talking. Some of the dancers are sitting in laps. I grit my teeth. That's breaking the no-touchy rule that's pretty bloody well known in strip clubs around the country.

This really is the personification of my father's internalised homophobia. The man was minted. He could have made a really classy joint. Something fabulous and exciting. Instead, it was like he crawled down here whenever he wanted to play in the dirt and dragged everyone else down with him.

"Paul," a slightly breathless voice calls over the music that's still reasonably loud, just not booming anymore. A cute guy in his mid-twenties dashes over. He's wearing booty shorts and a harness, and usually my interest would be piqued. But not tonight. Tonight, I'm feeling like the punchline of a bad joke, but it's even worse because all the people working here are in trouble as well.

It'll be fine. I'll fix it up, get it making a profit again, then sell it on. Like Paul, I'm starting to feel the need to look after this place. I don't *want* it. But I'm not going to abandon it, either.

"What's up, Tye?" Paul asks. The younger man does look a little flustered.

He glances between me and Paul, then fixes on Paul. He's the man he knows, after all, so I'm not slighted that he still sees him as the boss. I'm not sure I'd be able to help him with whatever his problem is anyway.

"There's someone asking at the bar for help with—uh—you know. A *room.* And there's a few drunk guys in the corner over there getting too handsy."

Paul fluffs up like an enraged pigeon. "I'll deal with that, if that's okay, boss?" he says to me with a nod towards the corner. Oh, fuck. Yeah. There are three guys who have clearly already had enough, and they're groping at a pretty boy in sequins.

"Yes, thank you," I say, not dreaming of getting in Paul's way. Yep. It's not the club or the business he's protective over. It's the employees.

I'm starting to like Paul a lot.

"I'll deal with the guy at the bar," I say, but he's already marching over to the louts, signalling for one of the bouncers.

Fine. If that's sorted, it's time for me to tell whichever suit it is that I'm no longer *whoring* anyone out.

Don't get me wrong. I'm one hundred percent for legalising sex work and unionising workers for their protection. But this isn't a safe environment, and I'm shutting that side of the business down right the fuck now. I don't care how much cash he's waving. One of the perks of being a trust fund baby is that I'm liquid enough not to have to stoop that low. I'll inject my own funds into this place as a loan, all above board, and pay myself back once it's earning again.

The bar is on the right-hand side of the stage. As I walk purposefully over, I can see Paul dealing with the grubby drunks from the corner of my eye. That's already pissed me off, so I'm not feeling very generous as I enter the bar behind the counter and scan the waiting customers.

I don't see any smug pricks in Savile Row threads waving around hundred-pound notes, though. Mind you, in this place, it could be the guy in tracky bottoms with a twenty sticking out from his tobacco-stained fingers.

Except he catches one of the bartenders' attention and is happy to order a rum and cola. No one else seems to fit the bill of what I'm looking for, so I approach the other bartender as he pours a glass of red wine.

"Someone was asking for me?" I ask as the music cranks up again, indicating a new act has climbed onto the pole. The server nods and points to the person waiting for me.

It takes me a second to realise who he means.

My heart flips.

The man is young. Not so young I feel the need to kick him out, but he's a baby, nonetheless. Maybe he's older than he appears, but his oval face is soft, and his brown eyes are wide as he nervously looks around the club. His hair is ridiculously thick, standing up proudly atop his head and curling around his ears.

I want to grab it.

Whoa. Fucking hell. *Down, boy.* I was ready to tear this arsehole a new one a second ago. He's still asking about one of those grotty rooms, isn't he?

Maybe there's been some kind of misunderstanding.

Whatever the case, this isn't what I was expecting at all.

3

CHARLIE

I'M TRYING TO LOOK LIKE I'M NOT OBSESSING OVER everything or that I'm so nervous I'm going to vibrate out of my skin. I hug myself in my damn hoodie. Luckily the bus was warm, so I dried off a little from the rain, but I'm still a dishevelled mess.

It took me a full half an hour to talk myself into coming inside Bootleg. I never have before, not even for a peek. But everyone knows this is where you come for the under-the-counter stuff. I've read stories online of what you can get up to in the backrooms.

This is the place for me to get my life back on track.

I attempt not to examine how depressing that thought is.

Someone else joins the bartenders on the other side of the counter. I try not to stare, but *holy fuck*. He's gorgeous. Like… he should be an actor or a model *gorgeous*. I wasn't sure what to expect when I asked for someone to help me with a problem. A manager or something. I suppose I was maybe envisioning someone a little grubby. Like the rest of this place.

Certainly not a lost cast member from Alexander McQueen's spring collection.

I realise he's looking at me as he talks to the bartender I spoke to previously. My heart rate feels like it triples, and despite getting soaked to the skin earlier, my mouth suddenly feels like the Sahara.

Then he's walking over. *Fuck, fuck, fuck!* He's frowning at me, like I'm a curiosity.

Because I am. Oh, *god!* This was a stupid idea! I have to get out of here! I have to—

"Can I help you?" he asks smoothly over the music that just got louder. Typical.

I guess he's mid- to late-thirties. He's wearing a white shirt and soft blue jeans, both of which cling to his muscular form. The top few buttons are undone, revealing a smattering of dark hair on his chest. His sleeves are rolled up to his elbows, showing off a few tattoos. I can't tell what they are without staring, but I can say with the utmost certainty that I want to lick them.

Focus!

"I, uh..." I mumble. "Who are...?"

He shakes his head and smiles. Holy *fuck,* that smile. It's like a toothpaste advert brought to life.

"Sorry, I should have said. I'm Miller Soldi. I recently took over ownership here at Bootleg." He checks his watch. "About two hours ago," he adds with a laugh that turns my tummy to butterflies. "I was told you asked for a private room, but I think there's been a misunderstanding. We don't offer anything like that here."

I glance around at the closed doors I clocked whilst I've been sitting here getting sideways looks for not ordering anything since I arrived. I should have asked for some free tap water, but I was too afraid in case they only had bottled and I would have to embarrass myself by declining. But yeah. Those doors. I was so sure that was going to be where I could do the…*thing.* I try not to tremble as perspiration breaks out down my neck.

Oh, god. There's probably some secret code, isn't there? I *know* this is the place to go if you want to buy sex. Therefore, it's got to be the place to sell sex as well, right?

I rub my hands together. There's no way I can play it cool, but I can at least try not to full out panic. "I n-need…" I stammer over the throbbing baseline.

He raises his eyebrows, then leans in, showing he can't hear me. Humiliation washes through me. I feel so stupid. This was a *bad* idea! I should just go. Yeah. Sleeping outside suddenly sounds a *lot* better than prostrating myself in front of this god-like man.

"S-sorry," I utter, trying to stand up from the bar stool. "I should just—"

The guy shakes his head impatiently, and a sickening feeling slithers through my gut. He's mad at me. Or…wait. He points at me, indicating I should stay put, then walks back around the bar.

"This way!" he shouts over the music once he's joined me, waving his hand, telling me I can move again.

Oh, fuck. Is this it? Is it happening? Am I about to get fucked?

I curse myself for being an idiot, then hurry up and follow him. He doesn't even know what I want. Just because I *wish* this guy could be the one to pound my virginity out of me, in no way does it mean that's what's going to happen. Besides, he might be hot, but he's probably a wanker. He owns this place, after all.

But then I think about that kind smile, and I'm not so sure.

He takes me to an office and shuts the door. I don't know if the walls are insulated or what, but the volume from the club drops immediately, and I can't help but breathe a sigh of relief. That makes things a little easier.

The place is a dump, but what's funny is that the guy also looks around at the stacks of old papers and dead pot plants with equal horror.

"What the fuck happened here?" he grumbles under his breath.

I try and hide a grin as he approaches the desk covered in many things, including a computer that looks like it's from the last century. It probably is. But I sober up pretty quickly when I remember why I'm there and what the hell I need to ask. Even worse, now I need to try and discover a secret code to get what I want.

Yep, there are the sweaty palms and dry mouth again.

"Right," he says as he moves some folders from the chair on the other side of the desk and drops into it. A little cloud of dust puffs out of the cushion, but he smiles that dazzling smile at me again like everything's fine.

It will be. I just need to keep my courage up.

"What can I help you with, Mr…?"

I shake my head. Gio made me take his stupid name when he married my mum, and since she and Dad are both dead now, I feel like I can't reclaim my old surname either. "It's just Charlie," I manage to rasp.

He nods. "Then you can call me Miller," he says kindly, touching his hand to his chest.

I swallow. Oh, yeah. He did tell me his name, but I promptly forgot. I kind of wish he'd given me his surname again now, though. He feels like he should be addressed as a Mr something.

"Okay, thank you," I manage to say without tripping over my words. "I need…I mean, I heard…" I take a deep breath and exhale, closing my eyes for just a second. *I can do this!* "I was told that this was the place to come to help me make an arrangement. A deal."

His eyebrows slowly crawl up his forehead. "This is a bar," he says sceptically. "If you're looking for a job, I'm afraid we're not hiring right now. In fact, we're about to go through a major shakeup, so I definitely can't take on anyone new. Servers or dancers or anything."

I'm really trembling. "No, uh," I whisper, unable to look him in his blue eyes. They seemed so warm a second ago, but now they're hard again, like when he arrived behind the bar. Like tropical waters that have now turned stormy. "I mean, yes, I'm looking for a job. For work. But not like that. I was hoping you could…if you knew someone…or how." This is going so badly. "I'd give you a cut," I blurt out.

Yeah. I sound like a lunatic.

He's looking distinctly unamused now. He laces his fingers together on the desk. "This isn't that kind of establishment," he says coolly.

Except I know it is! Fuck!

"I'm sorry!" I cry, fighting back tears. "I don't know the code word to use or the right thing to say! But what I'm offering…it's for the first time. Do you see? I just want to find someone who'd be willing to pay good money for that sort of thing."

He swallows, and there's something tense dancing in the air between us. I truly start to doubt that I've come to the right place after all.

"Anyone who would pay to do that to you is deranged," he says, his voice dangerously low, his hands still clasped in front of him.

He's glaring at me like I just asked to piss on the floor. I'm really shaking now and feeling sick.

Yeah, he's right.

I was *insane* to think that my virginity would be worth anything to anybody except me.

I open my mouth to tell him I'm not really looking for special treatment. Regular rates will be fine. Just *some* cash so I can get myself out of this mortifying situation and find somewhere to sleep tonight. That seems off the table now, though. Maybe I can at least find a different bar with a phone charger. A lot of places do that. Then tomorrow I can start again, and things will be better.

"Deranged, yeah," I croak.

Someone that beautiful probably looks at the likes of me and just sees a cockroach. I bet he lost his virginity when he was way younger than me. I bet it was spectacular.

He most certainly didn't have to sell himself to the highest bidder.

"I'm sorry I wasted your time," I manage to utter, walking backwards and fumbling for the door handle. "Have a nice night."

He's still looking murderous as I stumble back out into the club.

So I let the door slam shut behind me, then lose myself in the crowd.

4

MILLER

WHAT THE FUCK JUST HAPPENED?

Did that adorable boy just come into my club, into my office, and ask me to help him whore himself out to some sick fuck who wants to pay to pop his cherry?

Was that it? Did I get all the pertinent details?

Jesus fucking Christ. What kind of diabolical establishment did my old man bring to life here? More to the point, what kind of place now has my name signed across the bottom line?

I'm trembling with such rage that it takes me far too long to realise that he's gone. I was so appalled by what he was suggesting that I didn't think about what him leaving would mean.

He's gone off alone to try and find someone to pay him to fuck him for the first time.

I launch from my chair and throw myself at the door, yanking it open and flying into the club. He's got a few minutes' head start thanks to my stupid hesitation and inability to process beyond my rage and horror. The idea of that sweet boy…

I mean, there's a part of me that knows it's his body and he can do what he wants with it. But is that *really* what he wants?

I skitter out the front door onto the street. It's still raining, and I squint as I look up and down the ally. We're off the beaten track here, but I can't see anyone that looks like the boy—Charlie—in either direction.

Belatedly, I realise there's a bouncer watching curiously from under the small cover over the doorway. My bouncer. I click my fingers. "Hey—Dev, wasn't it?"

His face lights up, and I thank my mother for my manners. I bet my father never remembered this guy's name even once. "Yes, Mr Soldi, sir. How can I help?"

"Did you see a young man come out here? A bit shorter than me. In a hoodie. Ridiculous hair." I wave my hand a few inches above my own head to illustrate Charlie's luscious locks.

But Dev shakes his head. "No, sir. Sorry. No one's left the building since Mr Paul, um, *helped* those gentlemen leave."

The gropy drunks. Right, that's good at least. And if Charlie didn't leave…

I clap Dev on the back. "Good man. If you *do* see him, try and keep him here and call me. Understood? I'm going to look inside now."

He probably thinks I'm acting bizarrely, but Dev just nods. "Right you are, sir," he says. "Good luck," he adds like he's not quite sure what he's wishing me, but I appreciate the sentiment anyway.

"Cheers," I say, barrelling back inside and scrubbing my face with my hand, feeling the prickle of the neatly trimmed stubble I tend to wear.

I'm a fucking idiot. I let my pride overwhelm me, not to mention abhorrence of what such a pure soul was asking of me. I didn't think about *why* he was asking. I was just so determined to deny that's the reputation this place had until all of thirty minutes ago, when I changed it. I probably made that boy feel like a fool, or worse, a dirty criminal.

There's still time, though. Hopefully, I can fix this.

No one may have left, but at least a dozen more people have entered since Paul was showing me around. Bootleg isn't that big, and the extra bodies make a difference as I scan the room, looking for the mop of chestnut-brown hair. There's another couple of dancers on the stage, working the poles, and they're getting quite a reaction as they gyrate together. Between the music and the noisy crowd, I can't hear myself think.

I don't need to think, though. I just need to *look.*

"Come on, come on," I mutter, flexing and curling my fingers as my eyes dart over all the patrons and staff.

There.

For a second, I'm just relieved. That's definitely Charlie.

Then I realise that he's got his back against the wall. Some guy in a suit is looming over him, one hand braced on the wall by Charlie's ear, the other holding a tumbler full of whiskey that's dangling precariously from his fingers.

Charlie looks like a helpless little kitten who's been cornered by a bulldog.

I see red.

"I'm not sure," Charlie is saying with a wince as I approach. The guy has his back to me, but the music dips at the right time, so his voice travels.

"Now, now. Don't be a prick tease," he says roughly. "That sounded like a fun idea you had there."

"Can I *help* you?" I snap, yanking his shoulder and spinning him around probably far too roughly than I should. I don't give a damn about the rules right now, though. I made this mess, so I'm damned well going to fix it.

"Oi," says the suit, sloshing whiskey over his hand. "This is a private conversation. Fuck off."

I give him a tight smile. "And I own the place. So how about *you* fuck off."

I jerk my thumb towards the door. He glowers mulishly at me for a few seconds, then rolls his eyes.

"Whatever," he says with a curled lip. Then he looks Charlie up and down like he's a piece of shit. I'm tempted to slug him, but once he turns around, he's gone from my mind.

All I care about is Charlie.

"I'm sorry," he squeaks as I turn back to him. He's got his hands up. "I'll go. I'll leave."

"So you can just try this stupid idea on the *street?*" I bite out.

He sucks in a breath. Shit. I'm not trying to scare him, for crying out loud.

"Please don't call the police," he whispers.

Fucking hell. I'm acting like a brute and scaring him whether I intend to or not. I pinch the bridge of my nose. Of course another dancer takes to the pole, so the music cranks up again, making a delicate conversation nigh on impossible.

I grab his arm. "Come on," I say, pulling him back towards my office. He looks miserable, but we can't talk out here, and I'm worried he's going to bolt if I don't physically restrain him.

The idea of him approaching some sleaze down a back alleyway who's even worse than Mr Whiskey chills my blood and makes me want to break things. So he'll put up with a little forcefulness from me if that's what it's going to take to keep him safe.

"I'm sorry," he's spluttering again as soon as my father's office door is closed. It's not my office yet, and even when I clear it out, it won't be mine for long. But it's a quiet space away from the thundering baseline, so it'll do for now.

"Why?" I release my grip and look down at him. I'm not especially tall, but I'm glad I can use the slight difference to my advantage now.

He frowns at me. "Because you told me this wasn't that kind of place, but I'm sure it *is,* so I went asking around anyway. But then that guy smelled funny, and he wouldn't back off and—"

"No," I cut him off. "Not why are you sorry. Why are you *doing this?*"

He blinks up at me with spiky wet lashes. His cheeks are slightly flushed, and his breathing is raged.

My god, I just want to hold him until all his pain melts away.

That's not appropriate, though. I have a feeling I've walked into a minefield here, and I'm not taking another step until I get my bearings.

"What do you care?" he asks, a raw, harsh edge to his words.

"You're in my bar," is the easiest answer. Certainly better than 'because I've somehow convinced myself you're my responsibility'. And *way* better than 'because the idea of you selling yourself when you clearly don't want to is breaking my heart'.

Yeah. Now who sounds like a psycho? I'll keep that particular crazy emotional talk to myself, thank you very much.

"I'll leave," he says, but he's lost what little fight he had.

I step closer, crowding him.

He doesn't move away.

"Why?" I repeat.

Oh…fuck. His face crumbles. "Because I've got *nothing!*" he yells at me as a sob rakes through his chest and tears tumble down his soft cheeks. "No money, no food, no clothes, no bed! My stepdad threw me out, and I didn't know what to do and it's *raining* so—"

"Shh, shh," I say. I can't bear the anguish in his voice. It's killing me. Before I can stop myself, I'm pulling him against my chest, wrapping him in my arms as he wails and trembles. "Charlie, I'm so sorry that happened to you. That's unforgivable."

For a few minutes, I just let him cry. It feels like a lot more than just one night of grief that's pouring out of him. I'm not usually a huggy-feelsy sort of person, but it seems totally natural to just stand there with him and let him sob his heart out.

Eventually, he comes up for air, dragging shaky breaths into his lungs. I pull a handkerchief from my back pocket. "It's clean," I promise as I offer it to him.

He hiccups and looks at it for a second before taking it with a grateful nod. He rubs it against his eyes then blows his nose. "I'm sorry," he whispers.

I shake my head and brush my thumb against his cheek, catching the last of his tears. Fuck me. Where's all this *tenderness* coming from? I don't know this boy. I don't owe him anything. And yet there's something feral growling in my chest that says he's *mine* now.

"No, *I'm* sorry," I insist. "We got off on the wrong foot. How about we start again? I'm Miller."

I grin at him, hoping to lighten the mood. I'm stupidly relieved when he cracks the tiniest smile back in return. "That's the third time you've introduced yourself," he says with a shy sweetness.

I rub the top of his arm. "Let's make it the last as well, then. Hey, Charlie?"

He blinks those big eyes at me, still trembling like a little kitten. "You remembered my name?"

I almost scoff but manage not to. Something tells me that not many people remember this adorable boy's name.

They're obviously all morons.

"Of course I did," I say gently. "So let me get this straight. You were desperate for money, so you were trying to do something drastic?"

"And idiotic," he says with a roll of his eyes. "Like anyone would pay special rates for a first time with some penniless wretch. That's like something out of a Dickens novel."

I can't help but let my mouth twitch with a smile. "I must have missed that particular one in English class."

"Me, too," he says sadly. "I wish I knew how it ended."

Well, if I hadn't made my mind up before, I have now.

"I don't know about the *end*," I say with raised eyebrows. "But I can maybe help with the next chapter."

"Yeah?" he says sceptically.

"How does food, a shower, and a bed all to yourself sound?"

Yeah, I know. I'm a sap.

He just stares at me for a second. "What?" he eventually croaks.

I laugh softly and rub both his arms. He's still clutching my hanky and staring up at me like he's trying to work out if I'm an hallucination. Don't get me wrong. This white knight bullshit has got me questioning my sanity as well, but there's no way I'm letting this sweet young man walk out on me now.

"I'm offering you my spare room until you can sort yourself out," I say, looking into his brown eyes, making sure he doesn't flinch away. "You shouldn't have to do something you'll regret just because you fell on bad times."

His lower lip trembles. Then it's his turn to ask, *"Why?"*

I shrug and look away, just for a second. Because I feel guilty for kicking him out earlier? Because I'm mad at my

26

own father, and whilst I can't get back at him, I can thwart Charlie's arsehole of a stepfather? Because I'm a terrible man and can't deny that I'm attracted to this boy and want to keep him around a little longer?

"Because it's the right thing to do," I say eventually.

He bursts into tears again. "Thank you," he whispers as I hug him tightly once more.

Yeah. I'm not letting this little kitten out of my sight. Not until he's back on his feet again, anyway.

5

CHARLIE

I'D WORRY I WAS ON DRUGS, BUT I'VE NEVER TOUCHED THEM, and I don't intend on starting now.

Maybe this is a crazy fever dream? That would make more sense than it being reality.

I came into Bootleg looking to strike a deal to sell my virginity to some stranger. Instead, I'm sitting in the back of a fancy car being driven through London streets that I've only seen from buses before. Soon, we're driving west through streets that I'm certain I've never seen at all, neither in a bus nor a car. The area is far too posh.

Miller—I finally remembered his name—got me to wait in his office whilst he 'sorted some things out'. I wasn't sure what that entailed precisely, but if it meant a roof over my head, I was prepared to wait for hours.

He was back in under twenty minutes, though. He said goodbye to someone called Paul, asking him to call in case of emergency. He also said goodbye to the bouncer, calling him by his name as well. The guy—Dev—gave me a strange, knowing smile. I don't really know what that means, but it made me feel pretty good.

Now we're driving to wherever Miller lives. He asked if I liked Thai food, and I nodded, even though I'm pretty positive I've never tried it. I'll eat anything that's put in front of me right now, I swear. He doesn't elaborate on why he asked, though, and I don't ask.

I'm still absolutely convinced this is all going to blow back in my face. This insanely hot guy has no reason whatsoever to be kind to me. People never do anything for free, no matter what they might say.

But if there really is food and shelter, I'm still open to my previous idea of payment. Miller seems nice. Scary, but nice. Definitely a massive improvement on that guy with the whiskey breath back at the bar. I shudder. Yeah, if Miller wants that kind of gratitude, I think I can be brave enough to give it.

The drive doesn't take all that long, even though the traffic is pretty much what you'd expect for central London on a Friday night. That adds to my suspicion that Miller is filthy rich if he lives this close to central.

Such a vast chasm between our wealth makes me uncomfortable, especially when I literally haven't got a penny to my name. I keep swaying between deep relief for his help and a frightening gratitude that I could never even think about reciprocating.

But I need to, though. The power he has over me is shocking. I'm at his mercy. I'm really just trusting that he's being altruistic and that he's not actually some secret serial killer.

I'm not strong enough, though, to make it alone on the streets of the city. I'd rather take my chances on the kindness of a stranger. At least his breath doesn't stink of stale booze.

We arrive—or at least we come to a halt—down a long street of town houses. Miller thanks the driver by name once again and opens the door to slide out. Thankfully, it's stopped raining. Then…oh my god…he *holds his hand out for me.* To help me stand. Like I'm a princess or something.

I'm so flustered I don't know what to say. It's all I can do to stop myself from tripping over as he leads us towards one of the houses. By the time I think to say thank you, I feel like it's been too long since he let me go, and I'll make it awkward now.

I'm chewing my lip and pulling at my fingers as he unlocks his door. I glance over and see the car leaving. The house is three stories high, and I get a swoopy feeling just looking at it. The hallway beyond the door is narrow, so he enters first, then beckons for me to follow him inside.

When the door closes and we're properly alone for the first time, I know I need to make my move before I chicken out.

"Food's on the way," he's saying as he drops his keys into a bowl on top of a slim chest of drawers. It may have been wet today, but it was warm, and he didn't wear a jacket from the club. He slips his shoes off, though, and begins to head down the hall. "I can show you around in the meantime. This is—"

I catch his wrist, and he immediately stops to turn and look at me, his blue eyes wide with surprise. "Miller," I rasp, only daring to look him in the eyes for a second before flicking my gaze away. "Thank you."

"Oh, it's fine. Come on," he says jovially, but I jerk my hands forwards and fumble with the top of his jeans.

Now it's his turn to grab both my wrists, but his grip is a lot tighter than mine was.

"Charlie, stop," he says in a firm voice. For some mortifying reason, that tone goes *straight* to my balls and sends a shiver over my entire body. I peek up at him through my lashes. "What are you doing?"

I swallow. "Thanking you," I say. "You didn't have to do any of this, and I came to you with a proposal, so—"

"Whoa, whoa, *whoa,*" he says, gripping my hands harder.

And *that* bloody excites me as well because apparently, I'm a freak. But I'm not scared by his forcefulness. If anything, it makes me feel *safer* for some crazy reason.

"No, Charlie," he says, ducking his head and making me look him in the eyes. "You don't owe me anything. Least of all sexual favours. No. Please. Just..." He grimaces. "I don't know what's brought you to this point in your life, but you're safe now. We're going to have dinner and sleep, and then tomorrow we can work out what you can do next. I've actually got a lot of work-related decisions to make myself. So we'll get through it together. As a team. Let's try being friends, okay?"

I lick my lips, torn between heart-aching relief and soul-crushing mortification. Of course he wouldn't be interested in me sexually. But I got myself all geared up for the idea of finally going through with it, and he seemed like such a nice option.

But he's right. I don't *have* to do anything like that. Not tonight. And it's silly of me to think I'd be his type. He's such a commanding toppy kind of guy. He probably wants someone challenging.

None of that is stopping him from being kind, though. If I take a step back and just breathe, I'll see how much better that is than a one-night stand.

Even if he is hot as sin.

I compose myself and nod. "I'm sorry."

"You say that a lot," he tells me with a grin. And suddenly I know that everything's okay.

"Yeah," I agree meekly.

I expect him to release me then. But instead, he rubs his thumbs gently on the inside of my wrists, sending the most delicious sparks flying through my body. My lips pop open with a little breathless noise, and I look up at him again.

There's something different in his eyes.

It feels like heat.

I know I'm just a damsel in distress falling for this white knight, but I can't fight the way my heart is racing right now. He smells amazing and his grip is so firm. I just want him to pin me against the wall, but I'm terrified of what on earth I'll do if he does. Hell—I've never even properly *kissed* a man before. I've got no clue what to do, and I'll definitely embarrass myself awfully.

But it's like I'm being held prisoner by his gaze. Like I'm locked in a trance. If I just leaned in, his mouth is *right there...*

Thank Christ there's a knock at the door.

I jump back, and he blinks for a second before laughing. "That'll be dinner," he says, turning towards the door.

Am I hallucinating, or were his cheeks a little pink, and was his voice a little breathless?

No. That's crazy. He doesn't fancy me. He's just being a good Samaritan.

Right?

6

CHARLIE

I watch as Miller thanks the delivery guy and takes the bag of food, then closes the door and locks it.

Shutting the rest of the world out.

My two wrestling thoughts are, first, that I'm safe and, second, that we're *alone*.

"The tour might have to wait, I'm afraid," he says with a lopsided smile, holding up the bag. "I'm starving. Are you all right just to head to the kitchen?"

I nod, sure that if I open my mouth, I might squeak.

It looks like there's an office and a loo downstairs. He takes me up to the first floor, where there's a living room to the left. We head right into the gorgeous, massive kitchen with a breakfast bar that's so big it's practically a dining room table. I wonder who usually occupies the six stools.

I used to go round friends' houses to play when I was little, and to watch movies or do homework when I was a teenager. But since Mum got ill, all my social life just drifted away. Not that I really minded. Her health was absolutely my priority and I'll be forever grateful that I got to spend as much time as possible with her before she passed. But I've never been to anyone's house as an adult, and I certainly haven't been to one that they own all by themselves. It's intimidating, but it's also pretty awesome.

"I like your home," I say as he indicates for me to sit at the bar.

He smiles, and it's warm again, making my insides feel like they're full of sunshine. "Thank you. I've worked pretty hard on it, getting it just the way I want. Almost all the rooms have been completely remodelled since I moved in."

I skirt my eyes over the sleek cabinets and fancy-looking appliances again. "You decorated yourself?"

He laughs as he gets two plates out of a cupboard. "Well… I had a heavy hand in the designing, and then I *paid* someone with actual skills to do the hard work." He winks at me, making my tummy flip. "That's basically the same thing, right?"

"Right," I agree with a shaky smile.

He's pulling out numerous cartons from the brown paper bag. "I got a selection of things. Whatever we don't eat now can be lunch tomorrow if you fancy. And if you don't like something, please don't feel obliged to fake it."

I choke on nothing, thinking about how I was prepared to fake it for something incredibly intimate only an hour ago.

He raises his eyebrows, apparently unaware of my embarrassing thoughts. "Oh, damn. Let me get you some water."

He fetches a couple of glasses and fills them from a spout on one of the fridge doors—because it's so big, there are two. The water is chilled, and I sip it gratefully.

"Can I offer you something stronger as well?" he asks with a grin, opening the aforementioned massive fridge. "Beer? Wine?"

My heart skips a beat. Like so many things, I haven't had many opportunities to go out drinking over the past few years, and I never felt comfortable doing it at home with Gio around. That sounds like a good idea to shut my worries and nerves up right now, though. Also, I know it's stupid, but I kind of want to prove to Miller that I'm an adult, like him. Well, not *exactly* like him, with his fancy house and stuff. But that I'm…you know…not a child just because I'm a virgin.

However, I've never liked beer, and wine is so heavy. I consider for a second, trying not to overthink it.

"Um, that would be lovely," I say, plucking up some courage. "But do you have any spirits?"

His grin gets bigger, apparently delighted with my answer. I can't imagine why, but it makes me feel like I've won a prize or something. "Plenty," he says happily. "As well as loads of mixers. What's your tipple?"

I try not to fidget too much. "Oh, um. What's in a piña colada? I like that."

The last holiday Mum and I ever went on was this cheap package deal to Tenerife. It was especially great because Gio couldn't get the time off work, so it was just the two of us. She was too sick to indulge much herself, but she encouraged me to try some new things, and that's where I discovered a love for the fruity, creamy cocktail.

I have a sudden flash of embarrassment, realising that's probably way too complicated to make at home, but Miller is already beaming at me.

"Excellent choice. It'll give me a chance to get my shaker out. I'm sure I have coconut cream in the cupboard. One second…" He's muttering to himself as he starts rummaging around. Then he glances over his shoulder at me. "Oh, please start eating. We don't want it to get cold."

Honestly, whenever his eyes are on me, it feels like a spotlight. I know it's not because I'm special or anything. He probably looks at everyone like that. But it certainly makes me feel all squiggly inside.

"Um, thanks," I say, looking at all the open containers. It's a little overwhelming. There is rice, curry, noodles, vegetables in a sauce, lumps of juicy meat, and crackers, all in different boxes and bags. I'm not sure where to start, so I just reach for a crispy roll thing, hoping it's okay to eat it with my fingers.

"I did a mixology course a while back," Miller says as he puts ice in a big silver cup, followed by white rum, pineapple juice, and coconut cream that he's measured in smaller silver cups that look kind of like shot glasses. "I never get to play around with it anymore, though, so this is nice."

He looks at me, but I have no idea what 'mixology' is. "Cool," I say eagerly, hoping that's okay. Also that I haven't got any pastry or vegetables in my teeth from the roll. But damn, it was yummy.

He smiles softly at me as he jams a lid on the big cup and shakes it vigorously. "Sorry, mixology is a fancy word for cocktail-making. I find it soothing. I imagine that's how other people feel about baking cakes, but that takes way too long for my patience. I think it's similar, however. I like making pretty, sweet things for other people to enjoy. I just don't get the opportunity very often."

I nod with real enthusiasm this time. "I get that," I say genuinely. I don't bake or make drinks, but I understand how good it can feel looking after someone else.

He pours the frothy concoction into a glass almost shaped like a figure of eight, then adds a paper straw and glossy cherry that bobs around on the top. "Your beverage, sir!" he cries, pushing it towards me with a flourish.

I giggle, feeling a little shy at the attention but also loving it. How can this be the same scary guy from the bar?

"Thank you," I say timidly. I lean forward and take a sip, embarrassed when a moan inadvertently escapes my throat. "That's, um, lovely," I say. What I mean is that it tastes like happiness. Or at least it reminds me of the last time I was truly happy, which feels like the same thing. But that's a little too personal to share with a stranger.

He pours himself some red wine, then finally sits at the breakfast bar with me. His eyes flick over the almost untouched food, and a flash of shame surges through me. I don't want him to think I'm ungrateful. I'm just overwhelmed.

But the moment's passed in an instant, and he's reaching for both the plates. "Shall I dish you up a little of everything?" he asks convivially, like it's no big deal at all.

But it *is* a big deal. I expected him to ask me what I wanted or suggest I try a particular thing. But the fact that he wants to take charge and make the decision for me causes something to unfurl inside my chest that's both totally unexpected and frighteningly precious. I *love* this feeling.

"Yes, please," I utter.

I sip my drink and watch as he carefully spoons out a bit from all the cartons and even puts a handful of the crackers on top as well.

"I didn't get anything spicy," he says as he places the dish in front of me with a fork. "But even so, it might be a little hot if you're not used to it. Please let me know if so. I have sour cream in the fridge that will cool it down."

He's right. The spices are quite warm. But I like it. It makes my tongue kind of tingly.

We don't talk much during dinner. However, it's a comfortable silence. Tiredness is creeping through me like a rock trying to drag me underwater. I only manage half my drink, despite how delicious it is. But I am able to put most of the food on my plate away and down all the water. By the time Miller starts putting the lids back on the tinfoil boxes, my eyelids are drooping.

"Come on," he says gently, getting to his feet. "Let me

show you to the guest bedroom, Kit—Charlie."

I blink at him, but I'm not sure what other name he was going to call me. Kit? Probably someone he knows. I try not to get jealous of some imaginary guy. That's ridiculous. Besides, I'm too exhausted to muster up much envy right now anyway.

Okay. If this is the guest bedroom, I almost dread to think what his master bedroom looks like.

One wall is a dark teal, and the rest are a light grey. The floor is made of wooden boards, but there's a plush blue-and-white rug at the foot of the bed, which itself is a big double with an actual headboard. The duvet and pillow covers match the teal wall, and there are several white scatter cushions. The bronze ceiling light and bedside lamps look like they're part of an intergalactic fleet.

A lump forms in my throat. I seriously thought I'd end up sleeping on the street tonight. Yet here I am, in the lap of luxury.

"It's gorgeous," I manage to whisper.

He lifts his hand, then hesitates before giving my shoulder a quick squeeze. The brief contact sends shivers all over my body. I know I shouldn't be greedy. He's made his boundaries very clear. But I wish it could have lasted longer.

"Make yourself at home," he says with a nod towards the attached bathroom. Bloody hell. I assumed that was a closet until looking more closely. I have my own bathroom. "There should be a new toothbrush under the sink, and you can help yourself to any of the products you like. You're a bit smaller than me, but I think I should be able to find you some pyjamas that will fit."

I turn to him, the word almost falling out of my mouth again. *Why?* Why is he being so fucking nice to me if he doesn't want anything in return? I don't get it, and it's making me want to lash out. I don't trust it.

But I want it.

So "Thank you" is all I'm able to rasp instead.

He gives me a lingering look that I'm not sure about. Is he considering my offer of payment after all? I kind of wish he would. But then he licks his lips and nods.

"You wash up. I'll put out a set of pyjamas for you on the bed. I'll also keep the door ajar. If you need anything— anything at all—you just shout, and I'll hear you. Okay?"

There he goes again. Taking charge and telling me what to do. It should feel patronising or suffocating, but honestly, it just leaves me glowing, and the prickly worries that were tormenting me fade away.

I don't have to second-guess everything. I can just thank my lucky stars that finally—*finally*—something has gone my way in life.

I take a deep breath and find my words. "Thank you, Miller. I really appreciate it."

There's that strange look again. But then he nods once more and vanishes out into the second-floor hallway.

I only have the energy to brush my teeth, vaguely wondering what kind of person just has brand-new spare toothbrushes lying around. Miller, I suppose. From the wrapping, I think it came free from first class on an aeroplane.

Of course he flies first class.

I'm almost disappointed when I come out of the en suite and find the pyjamas left as promised. I kind of wanted Miller to be there, too. But I guess this way is less complicated.

I need less complicated right now.

A glance into the hallway tells me he isn't there either. So I quickly get changed, turn off the lights, and crawl under the covers. Holy *fuck,* the mattress and pillows feel incredible. Like I'm being cradled by a plump cloud.

And that's when I burst into tears again.

It's like a wave that rushes up and crashes right over me out of nowhere. I think it's relief and disbelief and probably a bunch of other things that I can't identify right now.

I'm *safe*. I'm *warm* and *dry*. And I didn't have to do something awful with a guy I didn't know or like.

I like Miller a lot. And he might not fancy me or whatever, but he's kind and caring, and I feel overwhelmingly lucky to have crossed his path tonight.

A sudden weight at the end of the bed almost stops my heart. It's certainly enough to jerk me out of the sobbing that I'm trying to keep as quiet as possible. For a second, I think I've failed and Miller heard my crying and came to comfort me. But there's definitely nobody there.

No-one human, anyway.

A tail swishes as the weight moves up the bed. It's a cat. I've not had much experience with cats, personally, so I hold my breath, not sure what to expect.

I can't see much in the dark other than that she (I'm just going to guess she's a she) is a shorthair. I lay perfectly still as she marches right up the bed, then headbutts me as she rubs her face against mine. She's purring.

Something blossoms in my chest. Like I've been given a rare gift. "Hi," I utter softly, daring to gently stroke her back. She turns around, still swishing her tail, and marches back down the bed. Then she flops and hugs my forearm like a koala, burying her face against the back of my wrist.

And there she stays.

I swallow the last of my tears, feeling like I'm a boat that's just dropped anchor in choppy seas. "Thank you," I whisper to my new cat friend in the darkness.

After that, I fall asleep almost immediately. I don't know what tomorrow will hold. But right now, I'm okay.

I'm safe.

7

MILLER

I'M SO AWAKE IT'S PAINFUL.

I feel like I've walked into an alternate reality. Seeing the bar I'd inherited out of the blue was always going to be weird, but I'd never have guessed in a million years that this would be how my night was going to end.

I'm trying to be responsible. I really am. But Charlie is just so fucking adorable and innocent, and it's like he's screaming out to be taken care of. I've had vanilla relationships, but I must admit I do prefer a partner who enjoys being dominated. Seeing how Charlie bloomed when I took charge of him was breath-taking.

Even better was the way he melted when I took hold of his wrists.

Fucking hell, I almost leaned in to kiss him.

That would have been very, very bad. He's vulnerable. I've promised to protect him. And if he thinks he needs to pay me back in some physical way, that doubly, *triply* means I can't lead him on in any way. I don't want him prostituting himself to anyone, least of all me.

But what if he's just attracted to me? What if it's genuine?

No. Absolutely bloody not, Soldi. You're the responsible one here. That boy doesn't need a good dicking. He needs comfort and security, something he's clearly lacking in his young life.

How his own stepdad could kick him out and leave him penniless, I can't fathom. In fact, my rage threatens to boil over every time it crosses my mind. But I force myself to steer away from that line of thought. Fuck that bastard, whoever he is. However, much like that prick in the bar that I scared off, I don't really care about who hurt Charlie in the past or who might have hurt him in the present. My only concern is his future.

He's clearly never been given a break. I can do that for him.

And that firmly means everybody's cocks staying in their pants. Sex complicates *everything*. Charlie needs simple and easy right now. He's got to build his whole life back together.

I just have to behave.

My god, I'd wanted to hug him good night. It wasn't even in a sexual way. I just wanted him to have some real human contact for a moment. I doubt his stepdad was much of a hugger. I know that feeling all too well. My old man was colder than a dead fish with his affection. And Mum showed love in her own way, but it was mostly with words. She wasn't a fan of anything that might rumple her clothes or ours.

I ball up my fists and rub them against my eyes. The urge to go down the hall and wrap myself around that boy whilst he sleeps so nothing can threaten him is *strong*. But he's not mine. He can't be.

Even though I almost called him 'kitten' out loud.

It just slipped out—or almost did, anyway. How the hell would I have been able to walk that one back? I don't know why, but that's just the name for him that really wants to take up space in my brain. Like I see Charlie and my mind supplies 'kitten' all on its own.

Well, I do know why. He's trembling and adorable with huge eyes and a ridiculous amount of hair, exactly like a kitten. It's like I found him on my doorstep, abandoned in a box labelled 'Help me!'.

Thank god I was the one who found him. Thank god I got to him before Mr Whiskey could drag him off to some dark corner.

I feel my blood pressure start to rise again at the mere recollection of it, so I force myself to think calming thoughts as I breathe deeply in and out.

Charlie is safe. He's down the hall on a memory foam mattress with me and my front door standing between him and anything that might want to hurt him. I don't know how long he'll want to stick around, but as long as he does, he's going to be my responsibility.

He's mine.

I grit my teeth and try to stop the primal instinct from curling through me like intoxicating liquor in my veins. But it's wild and savage. It may have been a strange series of events that brought us together, not to mention that it only happened a few hours ago, but there's something so right about it my baser instincts can't fight it.

As a man, I might be able to resist and do the right thing to protect my little kitten's virtue.

But as a beast, as a carnivore, I want to rub my scent all over him and dare any fucker to try and come within ten feet of him. I want to snarl sharp teeth or bang my chest.

With my blood pumping like this, it's no wonder that I've got a throbbing hard-on. I'm doing my very best to ignore it because I promised myself that I would try to keep my thoughts pure when it came to Charlie. After all, that's what he is. Pure.

But I keep thinking about that moment in the hallway when he grappled with my jeans. The way he went so compliant as soon as I grabbed his wrists and made him stop.

What if I hadn't made him stop? Or...what if I'd lifted those wrists and pinned them against the wall? I can picture his eyes getting even bigger, his plump mouth popping open, just begging for me to ravish it. Or would he prefer a firm hold and extra-gentle kisses? Could I make him come undone from soft touches alone, I wonder?

I bite my lip, my fingers itching to take myself in hand as I let my mind drift.

When he says he's a virgin, what exactly does he mean? I don't like the idea of *anyone* having put their hands on him. They almost certainly wouldn't have done it right or taken the care and attention he clearly deserves. I find myself desperately hoping that he's completely innocent. That he's never tasted or even touched another man's cock.

I'd be so gentle. I'd go so slowly.

With a snarl, I give in and lick my damn hand before thrusting it under the sheets and pulling my briefs down so I can wrap my fingers around my shaft. I'm rock hard already, so I know it's not going to take long. And I promise myself that no one on earth ever needs to know that I gave in to temptation. I won't do it in real life, so a fantasy is harmless.

As my hand flies up and down my length, I picture how I would have kissed him tenderly in my entrance hall with his hands held firmly against the wall. He would have squirmed but in a good way. In delight. But the more I kissed him, the stiller he would have become, turning to putty under my body.

Then I would have carried—yes, *carried*—this is my bloody imagination—him up to my bedroom where I'm debasing myself right now. I'd have laid him down with care. Seeing as this is a fantasy, I scatter rose petals all over the bed in my mind's eye for good measure. Who cares how they got there? It's romantic as fuck, and my little kitten deserves to be swept off his feet.

I'd slowly peel all his clothes off and kiss every inch of that soft skin. I'd stroke his tummy and murmur sweet nothings until he no longer trembled in fear. My little scaredy-cat. I'd prove to him how safe he is now. Maybe I'd stretch him slowly with my mouth. Yes, and I'd touch his cock whilst I did. I bet it's pretty. His cock, which no one else has ever touched before.

Once he was ready, I'd take my time sliding into him. I'd have him on his back so I could look into his eyes as I penetrated good and deep, lighting him up once I found his prostate. Then I'd rock…and rock…and *rock*.

I bite my lip and gnash my teeth as I wank hard. I use my other hand to fondle my heavy balls and stoke my taint. God, I'd lose myself completely in that sweet, beautiful boy. I'd treat him right like I'm sure no one else would. He was desperate enough to throw his first time away on something seedy just to scrape enough cash together for a bed for the night.

I'd keep him in my bed forever and give him a first time that he'd cherish just as long.

I'm obviously high on my almost orgasm, but I don't fight it. In that moment, it feels perfectly natural that I'd keep him forever. A kitten is for life, after all, not just for Christmas. Fuck, he'd never want for anything ever again if he were really mine.

Mine.

Mine.

That's the word that blots everything else out as I groan as loudly as I dare with the door open and start splattering cum all over my hand. Charlie is *my* kitten, and I'll treat him better than he ever dared dream of.

Even as I start floating down, milking the last of my spend onto my belly, I picture myself kissing him after his first fuck. I'd cradle him as I softened inside, telling him how good he was and how proud I was of him. Then I'd carry him —yes, carrying again—into the shower, where he'd let me take care of cleaning him up so he'd be all comfortable to fall asleep in my arms.

Eventually, I'm wrung out. I release myself and grope for some tissues to mop up the worst of the mess. A shower in real life probably isn't the worst idea, but for a moment, I just lay there staring at the ceiling. I wait for the guilt to hit over what I've just done, but it never arrives.

In fact…the only feeling that creeps in is sadness. God, I wish I could bring that fantasy to life, but I never can. Absolutely never, no matter what Charlie might say or do. He's vulnerable and not in his right mind. What if he made a move and I followed through, only to discover that he was just offering himself up in some misplaced notion of repayment.

That turns my blood cold.

I puff out my cheeks. It's okay because I'll never let that happen. And try as I might, I really can't find it in myself to feel ashamed over my fantasy. It was beautiful. As I tear myself out of bed and into my en suite, I promise myself that I'll cherish it.

Just like I will whatever time I get to have with my little kitten.

8

CHARLIE

I'M HALF-AWAKE WHEN I HEAR A SOFT KNOCK AT THE DOOR. My first thought is to wonder where the hell I am. When the memories come flooding back to me of the evening before, I immediately look around for my new cat companion, sad that she's no longer wrapped around my arm. But she's there, curled up by my feet, and I feel a pang of gratitude. In the daylight, I can see that she's a tawny sort of colour with stripey legs. Almost like a little tiger.

Then I look up to see Miller watching me with such a warm expression that my heart skips a beat. He's in a set of pyjamas like the ones I'm wearing. Long, soft trousers and a T-shirt. But I can still see his muscular abs and arms, and my morning wood gets a little more excited under the covers than it already is.

"Um, hi," I croak, rubbing the sleep from my eyes. It's then I notice that he's got two mugs of tea in his hands.

He raises one. "I didn't know how you took it, so I made it like mine with dairy milk and no sugar. But if you want sugar or other milk, I can—"

"No, no, that's fine," I say as I sit up, ridiculously pleased that we take our tea the same way. I know logically it doesn't mean anything, but I'm still half-asleep, and knowing it sends warm tingles through my body. "Thank you."

He comes into the room but then immediately spies the cat who has raised her head. "Oh, Florence," he says with a tut. "I hope she didn't bother you," he says to me. "Bugger. I should have checked if you were allergic."

He hands me my tea, and I shake my head. "I'm not allergic and she didn't bother me at all. In fact, we had a lovely cuddle last night that helped me fall asleep."

He huffs, but the smile he gives his cat is full of love. Then…*oh god…*he sits on the end of the bed next to her, right next to my feet, giving her a stroke. "Did you sleep well?" he asks me.

My mouth has gone so dry I'm grateful to take a sip of tea. "Yes, thank you. Um, if you need me to leave, I can get going soon—"

"Whoa, whoa, Charlie," he interrupts. He's shaking his head with a frown, and I bite my lip as I wait for his next words. "No. I don't need or want you to leave. In fact, I'd like it very much if you stayed here as long as it takes to get you back on your feet. I don't care if that's weeks or months. I'm not kicking you out onto the street. I promise."

I let out a shaky breath. "I can't offer you rent," I say hesitantly.

He shrugs. "I don't need you to. The mortgage is paid, and I have plenty of funds. My father may have been a bastard, but he was a *rich* bastard. I got a good start in life and have worked steadily my whole life. So please stop worrying."

I take another sip of tea and roll his words over. It's scary to feel indebted to someone I barely know. But I can't deny the relief his words offer me. "I do have a job," I say, realising that I never told him that yesterday. "It's just part-time and doesn't pay much, but I was going to ask for more hours or something. But I'll need a new bank account that my stepfather can't access and—"

"Hey, hey," he says softly, reaching over to squeeze my knee through the duvet. Jesus, I'm really going to have a heart attack at this rate. "We can figure all that out later. I absolutely want to hear more about what your stepfather's done with your money, though. Because that sounds illegal."

"He, um, took everything," I say with a wince. "I think his name was on the account as well. I know he set it up for me years ago. But I was supposed to get my inheritance from my mum yesterday, except he cleared it out before I could touch a penny. I guess I could take him to court, but honestly, I hate him so much I don't know if I have the strength for that. I kind of just want to never see him again."

Miller's jaw is tight, and he stares at me for a second. "What a fucking dickhead," he growls.

It sends a delicious shiver through me, and I'm not quite sure why, so I cover it up with a nervous laugh. I guess I'm not used to people sticking up for me. Certainly not sexy men sitting on a bed with me. I always tried my best not to put my mum in the middle of me and Gio, but it was difficult. The man is a menace.

Was.

God, I'd be happy if I never saw him again. Even if it means I never see a penny of Mum's money.

"Why yesterday?" Miller's question cuts through my thoughts.

"Oh, um…it was my twenty-first birthday."

For some reason, I'm embarrassed. Probably because it was a really pathetic way to spend what's supposed to be one of the most important landmarks of your life.

Miller's head twitches, and his gaze narrows at me. "Yesterday was your birthday?" he says, something catching in his gravelly voice.

"Yeah," I say, rolling my eyes. "I went for a walk in the park, and when I came home, the locks had been changed. Fun."

I'm trying to make a joke out of it, but his eyes are blazing. "I'm going to fucking kill him," he says so low I almost don't catch it.

"Whoa, no," I say. This time it's my turn to reach out. I don't quite have the courage to touch him in any way, but I stop just short of that and wave my hand. "He's not worth it. Fuck him. I ended up spending my birthday with a really nice guy and trying Thai food for the first time and snuggling with a kitty to go to sleep in a safe, dry bed. At the end of the day, it was kind of great."

He stares at me, the moments starting to drag on, and it feels like something crackles between us. Then he nods stiffly. "I'm glad," he says eventually, looking into his tea. "Happy birthday, Charlie. I hope this is the start of a much better year for you."

I let out a little laugh. "Bloody hell. Me, too."

That seems to break the tension, and he laughs as well.

Right. Time to stop second-guessing everything and try a little trust. It's what Mum would tell me, I'm sure. She wouldn't want me to be reckless (and I pray if she's watching over me, she'll forgive me for the *insanity* I was considering last night), but I think I've been cautious enough with Miller.

"If you're really sure about me staying…" I say slowly. "Then thank you. That would be absolutely incredible."

He sighs and gives me another one of those warm smiles that makes me glow. "I'm one hundred percent sure. And whilst you're having a cash flow and bank account problem, I'll take you out shopping today for some clothes and essentials."

My stomach drops in horror. That's *way* too much. "Oh, no, I—" I splutter, but he shakes his head and raises a finger to quiet me. My stomach does that swoopy thing again when he takes command. Why do I find it so hot that he's telling me off?

"Nope. No arguing. It will take a bit of time to set you up a new bank account. Do you even have any ID?"

I hadn't considered that. "I've got my provisional driver's licence in my wallet," I say with some relief. I've never driven in my life, but I'm glad I got it precisely for identification purposes. Gio has my passport, and I'll have to consider what I'm going to do about that another day.

Miller nods. "Good. That's something at least. You won't have any utility bills, but some banks have specific accounts for people seeking refuge, so we can research the best one of those."

We. *We.*

I look down at my half-drunk tea and try to discreetly swallow the lump that's threatening to form in my throat. I still don't understand why Miller's wasting his time on some strange young man he met twelve hours ago, but something's urging me to just go with it. My stepfather might be a terrible man, but it stands to reason that there are *good* men in this world as well.

"I'll pay you back for everything," I try meekly, but he just flat out grins at that.

"No, you won't," he says cheerfully, reaching over to muss up my hair.

My heart almost stops. Seriously, he better have a defibrillator to hand. It was a playful gesture, but my cock has leaped to attention the moment I felt his touch.

"They're going to be birthday presents," Miller announces, sounding very pleased with himself. "So you're not allowed to pay me back."

There's no stopping the lump in my throat now. Nor the

tears that spring into my eyes. "Birthday presents?" I whisper.

I know it's ridiculous, but when Mum died, I kind of thought no one would ever buy me presents again.

His look is full of kindness and sympathy. He nods. "Yes, Charlie. I want to buy you some presents for your twenty-first birthday, if that's okay."

I just about manage to put my mug down on the bedside cabinet before I throw myself at him. He immediately wraps his free hand around my back and lets me bury my face against his neck. I try and keep the crying to sniffles rather than the full-blown sobbing I inflicted on him last night, but he doesn't seem to mind. He rubs my back.

"It's okay," he murmurs over and over.

I'm not sure it is, though.

How the hell am I going to survive living with this incredible man and not fall in love with him?

9

MILLER

It's a long time since I had such a domestic day. I've had relationships in the past—some of them lasting for a couple of years even—so I've been shopping with boyfriends, and a couple of them moved in here for a time. But there was something fundamentally different about my time spent with Charlie today.

We just went to the big shopping centre in White City. It's mostly made up of chain stores, so not what I'd call fancy, but he wandered around in a daze like I'd taken him to Disneyland.

It became apparent very quickly that he was too afraid to make decisions on anything, but what I honestly found more terrifying was the thrill we both obviously got from me taking charge and picking things for him. Naturally, I didn't force anything on him. There were plenty of things he considered, but I worked out fast when his face would light up for what he truly wanted.

I'm not supposed to be getting in this deep at all, let alone so fucking fast it's giving me whiplash. But his submission is painfully clear, and he evidently gets a lot of joy and peace from it that I doubt he's ever experienced before in his life. He doesn't even seem aware of it, in fact.

His obliviousness was probably what made me think it was okay to indulge. What he wouldn't know wouldn't hurt him, right? This way we could both have a lovely time, and—more importantly—he's now got a decent selection of clothes, toiletries, and a phone charger.

The beginnings of an independent life.

I treated him to lunch out and after I organised our many bags to be stored in a locker facility, I gave him the option of bowling or mini golf as the last part of his birthday present. I was really proud that he only hesitated for a moment before choosing mini golf. Neither of us were especially good, but we laughed.

A lot.

Now that we're home and I've made a risotto for dinner, it's really, *really* hard not to feel like we've been on a date. Especially as I've had the privilege of seeing Charlie become more and more relaxed as the day's gone on. He's got a couple of piña coladas in him as well that are making him sweet and giggly.

Sweet-*er* I should say. He's been adorable since the moment he woke up, looking all rumpled with my cat curled up by his feet. In fact, she's still hovering around him now. I'm sat on the sofa, and he's on the floor—yes, I noticed immediately that he put himself down there, quite happily—and we're going over some of his admin options, namely his new bank account.

It should have been boring, but it's not.

I've kept the conversation light throughout the day, but I think it's finally time to ask a difficult question. I don't need to know it to fill out the rest of this application for him, but I've got to the point where I can't fight asking because I need to know *him* better.

"Charlie," I say evenly. He's stroking Florence and looks up at me with those big, beautiful eyes.

"Hmm?"

"You said your inheritance was from your mum. Is that a savings account she set up?"

He bites his lip and looks down. I fucking hate dimming his sparkle, but hopefully, it won't be for long. And after this, I'll have more of the pieces to his puzzle.

"Yeah, when I was a baby," he explains sadly. "She contributed to it regularly when she was working, then what she could when she got sick, then…"

He screws his eyes up, and tears leak down his cheeks. Ah. I'd suspected as much. I reach over and squeeze his shoulder.

"When did she pass?"

He sniffs and scrubs his face. "Last year. Cancer. It was… really hard. And long. It's why my life seems so boring. Nothing was as important as looking after her. I kept hoping if I just loved her more, it would be enough. *Fuck* cancer," he adds savagely. My heart breaks for him.

"I'm so sorry, sweetheart," I say. The term of endearment slips out, but I can't say I regret it, and he doesn't seem to particularly react to it. I rub my thumb against his shoulder. "That was a lot to take on at such a young age. You were very brave and selfless. Were you her primary carer?"

He nods. "Anyone would have done it, though," he says with a little frown.

Oh, *kitten.*

I can't help it. My protective instincts flare like a roaring dragon. I'm amazed I manage to keep my voice calm, but I can't stop the words from coming out.

"So your stepfather helped as well, did he?"

He drops his head and looks at the floor.

That's what I thought.

"My dad was lovely," he says somewhat tangentially. "Or so Mum said. I've seen photos, though, and he's got a really nice smile. But he was killed in a car crash when I was a toddler. Mum was…she was wonderful, but she was kind of helpless. Insecure. My gran was pretty mean to her, so I think she was desperate for someone else to come along and take care of us both." He grimaces as he pokes at the morello cherry in his drink. "Unfortunately, it was Giovanni who came along. His version of 'taking care' of us was nothing more than bullying."

His face crumples again, and he wipes away fresh tears. I know I shouldn't, but I slide off the couch to sit beside him, wrapping my arm around his shoulders. Fuck, this is crossing all those lines I promised myself were sacred in bed last night. But he's in so much pain it would be completely wrong to stay away right now. I know it.

"I was going to leave yesterday," he carries on, calmer once more. I love that he's leaning into me. Like I can take some of that weight for him. "I was looking for a room of my own in a house share. I was going to take that money and be out of his hair for good. But he had to fuck me over one last time."

"No, he hasn't," I say firmly. "You're free of him and here now, and we're going to sort it all out."

He bites his lip again and turns those brown eyes on me. We're so close, sitting side by side. His breath ghosts over my skin as he looks at me imploringly. "You've been so kind, Miller. I really don't understand it. And I don't think I'll *ever* be able to repay it."

I sigh and shake my head. Here we go again with the repayments. "Because you're a good person who deserves good things, Charlie," I say with conviction. I give him a little poke with a smile. "And definitely *not* boring. It's my pleasure to help you in your time of need. I could slip from this mortal coil tomorrow satisfied that even if it's just for one person, I left the world better than when I entered it."

"Don't!" he squeaks fearfully, shaking his head and grabbing my shirt. "Don't say that. Don't talk about dying."

Idiot. I squeeze around his shoulders and use my other hand to cup the back of his head. "I'm sorry. I'm not going anywhere. I promise."

I know logically that I can't guarantee anything like that, but my words seem to mollify him. It's true that I can't control whether or not I get hit by a falling piano. But I'm not going to *leave* him. Not now, not for a long time. He needs me, like a baby bird.

But…he needs me *more* than that, I'm sure. As we sit there gripping tightly to one another, I feel him trembling, and I look into his wide eyes. There's a desperate heat there. He doesn't just need me for food or shelter.

He needs me for *me.* And I know that I'd take better care of him than anyone else probably could. He's in my veins now, under my skin.

But I can't. I fucking *can't.* It's immoral and irresponsible, and he literally just mentioned about repaying me again. Even though it's tearing me up inside, I ease my grip and start to pull away.

He jerks away like he's been hit by lightning.

"Charlie?" I say, baffled. I know I wanted to put the brakes on, but he's acting like he's just been burned.

"Sorry. I'm sorry," he croaks. "You said you didn't want that, and I keep throwing myself at you. You've been so kind. I don't want to mess it up. I'm stupid. I'm sorry—"

"Charlie, I need you to stop and take a breath," I say in my Dom voice. "I never said I didn't want to be close to you."

"Friends!" he cried. "You said *friends!* I'm so messed up. I'm being totally ungrateful and seeing things that aren't there. It won't happen again, I promise."

My insides flip. I think it's pretty obvious that he does want *me,* not just that he wants to use sexual favours to clear some imaginary debt. But he's so vulnerable. I have to treat carefully, *so* carefully.

"I hope we are friends now," I say, but he's not calming down. He's getting worse.

"I'm just a silly bloody virgin who keeps thinking I'm more important than I am! What's wrong with me? You're completely out of my league and just being nice!" He scrambles to his feet, and I'm at the wrong angle to follow him fast enough. "I'm sorry I ever bothered you. Thank you so much for all the shopping. I'll leave. I'll pay you back. I'll—"

I lose my patience and interrupt.

Except I almost use the wrong fucking name. Again.

"Kit—Charlie, no, stop, that's not—"

"Who's Kit?" he yells, throwing his hands out and shaking his head. "I'm getting delusional thinking I'm falling in love with you, and you can't even remember my name!"

And then he's gone, sprinting up the stairs to the second floor. I've finally managed to untangle my legs and follow in hot pursuit, but by the time I reach his door, he's not only slammed it shut but locked it.

I forgot it even had a lock. That was from the brief period I rented it out. *Damn it.*

"Charlie," I say miserably, leaning against the wood with my palms splayed wide like I can melt through if I try hard enough. "Please let me in. We can talk about it."

I feel something hit my calf. Florence winds her way between my legs, swishing her tail angrily, then headbutting me again.

"Yeah, yeah, I know I fucked up," I grumble at her. She meows angrily in response. "I'm fixing it," I tell her, hoping that's actually what I'm doing. Knowing my track record with Charlie so far, I'm probably just making it worse.

His voice is small as it comes through the door.

"Is Kit your boyfriend?"

My heart twists, and I lightly thump my head against the wood. "No, sweetheart. I don't have a boyfriend. I'm very single, and the only person I care about in this whole world right now is you. So will you please, *please* let me in?"

There's a long pause that I don't breathe for. "I want to know who Kit is."

I exhale, having to admire his spirit. He's not a pushover, for all life has thrown at him. He's got fight in him.

I give in. This has already gone way past the point of no return.

"You're Kit," I say softly. I hope it was loud enough for him to hear. Now I'm the one who's afraid, and I don't think I can repeat it.

I wait.

The lock clicks.

I take a step back, holding my breath again. The door slowly creeks open, and he looks up at me with wet eyes. "I'm Kit?" he says dubiously.

I nod. "I can explain." At least, I *hope* I can. "Can I come in? I think we've been talking at cross purposes. I don't want you to leave. I keep saying that, and I mean it."

He shrugs heavily. "People don't always mean what they say, do they?"

I bet he thinks that. I bet he's so tired of being kicked around by worthless shits like his stepdad. That makes my mind up.

Even if it ruins everything, I'm telling him *exactly* how I feel.

10

CHARLIE

I'M FEELING EMBARRASSED AND SHAKY AS I ALLOW MILLER into the room that he's so kindly given me for the time being. I'm also dizzy like I've had a nasty shock.

Well, I kind of did. I let my walls down and told him all about my dead mum, and then he pulled away from me. But then he said a bunch of other stuff, and…oh, I don't know anymore.

I don't understand how I can possibly be Kit, but I'm ashamed of how much I want to be.

Once he's come over the threshold, he watches me for a second. "May I hug you?" he asks.

I should say no, but I feel like I'm going to shake apart. So I just nod instead, gasping when he pulls me into a fierce embrace.

"I am *so sorry,* sweetheart. I promised to take care of you."

"You are," I say quickly. Because in truth, he's taken care of me better in one day than anyone else my entire life, even Mum, god rest her soul.

He shakes his head against mine. "I made you cry. That's unforgivable."

I let out a wet chuckle. "To be fair, I'm crying all the time right now. It's hardly your fault."

But he pulls away and—*holy fuck*—cups my face with both his hands, staring at me with those eyes like a stormy tropical sea. "No, Charlie. I tried to protect you, but that meant not being honest about my feelings. You're an adult, and I should have just told the truth rather than try and do what I think is best without explaining it all or consulting you. So I'm really sorry, and I hope you'll forgive me."

For a second, I forget how to breathe. Wow. That's...that's a lot.

"O-of course I forgive you," I stammer, bewildered as to why I wouldn't.

Now I've calmed down, I can see how unreasonable I was. In my defence, I think a lot of that might have been misplaced anger at Gio for his despicable treatment of me and at the universe for taking my mum from me so cruelly. So why should Miller apologise?

"Come here," he murmurs, taking me by the hand and leading me to the bed.

My heart's definitely going to give out on me this time. Forget CPR. It's just going to explode out of my chest. But he sits with his back against the pillows, then tugs me so I'm pressed against him, under his wing. Oh *god*, it feels so nice. I try and resist for half a second before I cuddle in closer.

"Good boy," he murmurs, and I melt.

File that under the growing header of 'Stuff I should find patronising, but it just turns me on and makes me feel super awesome'.

"I'm not sure where to start, so I'll go with the fact that *you're* Kit. It's not some secret or ex-lover. It's you."

I frown, hardly daring to believe it. "Why?" I ask, far calmer than every other time I've uttered that word in the past twenty-four hours.

He pauses so long I almost look up from where I'm clinging to his side. But then he squeezes me tighter and sighs.

"Because you're my little kitten," he says softly and almost sadly.

My insides drop out from within me but in the most wonderful way. It takes me a second to catch my breath and steady my racing heart. But then I swallow and finally do look up at him.

"I am?" I whisper.

He looks at me with such affection it makes me want to squirm. He brushes the backs of his fingers along my cheek, lingering just by my lips.

"Ever since I saw that brute corner you in the club. I felt wretched for scaring you off already, but that guy was a real sleaze, and you looked like a helpless kitten." He drops his hand to pick up one of mine, playing with my fingers. "But kittens aren't entirely helpless. They have claws and teeth. They can scratch and bite. You might be sweet and adorable, Charlie, but you've also got bite. I've seen it. So...yes. That's my secret. One of them. I've been thinking of you as a kitten. *My* kitten. But I didn't think it was appropriate. You were frightened and vulnerable, and I just wanted to help, not make things more complicated."

"More complicated, how?" I ask before I can think better of it.

He plays with my fingers some more, stroking them and sending shivers all over my skin. "You came to me offering yourself sexually to the highest bidder because you were in such dire straits. I was horrified...mostly because I didn't want anyone else putting their filthy hands on you."

I go still in his arms. "Anyone *else*," I manage to utter in disbelief, not daring to believe what I think he might mean.

But he squeezes my fingers before raising them to his lips and *kissing them.*

I think I might actually combust on the spot.

"My hands are actually very clean," he says, a touch of humour in his voice, but I'm still too stunned. "Not filthy at all. I promise."

"You…want me?" I say slowly.

"All to myself," he says heavily. "But I was worried you were only interested in me because you felt obliged, and I couldn't have that, not in a million years. So I shut you down."

I take a few shaky breaths. "I do feel like I owe you a lot," I say carefully. "But…no. I want you just for you, Miller. But I'm terrified I'll be no good."

"Oh, *kitten,*" he says, sounding so distressed. He shifts me against him, and I go with it, moving until we're face to face again. He shakes his head and caresses along my jaw, making me tremble. "You don't have to be anything other than yourself, okay?"

I look down the bed. I'm not sure when Florence jumped up and settled by our feet, but she's watching us now like she's trying to make certain we don't do anything stupid.

Again.

"I wish I really was a cat," I say with a scoff. "Then I might be more confident and stop second-guessing myself. Because I still have *no* idea why you would think I'm special."

I look back at Miller as he gives me a sad smile. "I know," he says with a soft laugh. "But you are, my Charlie kitten. Your kindness shines through on that beautiful face. I love how resilient you are. I've seen you at your worst, but then I saw you today, admiring all the sparkly things in the shops and doing silly victory dances when you got your golf ball in the hole. I think you're not used to hearing it, but you're lovely and precious, and if it's what you want, I'd really like to continue getting to know you. I want to keep helping you —and before you protest, helping you is something that makes *me* really happy. It's a bonus as far as I'm concerned. I want you to feel safe with me."

That's a lot to process, so I rest my head on his chest again and snuggle back close. "I feel safer with you than I have with anyone ever in my whole life," I confess. It's pretty scary to lay myself bare like that, but he's right. We've both been making assumptions about the other and dancing around admitting what's really going on, and it just got us hurt.

He rubs my arm and kisses my hair. "That makes me so, so happy, kitten."

I grin and bite my lip. "Me, too," I admit. "Um, just to be clear, though. I also think you're super hot."

He roars with laughter, and that makes me feel *amazing.* I love knowing I did that.

"You're hot, too, kitten," he says. "Just in case that wasn't obvious." I frown and glance up at him. But he knows I'm going to protest and rolls his eyes. "You are a fucking *morsel,* okay? You stole my breath the moment I saw you at the bar. You're beautiful like a cherub and that hair…" He laughs and shakes his head.

"What?" I ask, slightly nervous, patting it and wondering how unruly it's become.

"Exactly," he cries. "It's just so…it makes me want to…oh, fuck it."

He slides his fingers through it and grips tight, sending little shocks through my scalp and the rest of my body.

Particularly my cock. Oh god, why is that so *hot?*

I whimper and pant, suddenly aware of how close our faces are together. But I'm scared I'm going to fuck something up. "Miller?" I squeak, really feeling like a kitten.

"I'm right here," he murmurs, eyes searching mine as the moment stretches on.

"Please," I manage to utter eventually.

He crashes his mouth onto mine, and I swear my soul leaves my body. I don't know why I was so worried about not knowing what I was doing, because he's doing it all for me. Our lips mould together, and his tongue plunges between them, seeking mine out. His fingers massage and tug at my hair, and his other hand digs into my back as I cling to his chest.

Jesus fucking Christ. If I knew kissing was this amazing, I'd have tried harder to do it years ago. Or maybe it's best I didn't. Even without anything to compare it to, I know this is spectacular.

I'm so, *so* happy that this is my first proper kiss.

Eventually, I have to come up for air. I gasp and blink as I look into his eyes, which are filled with the warmth of my favourite smile but also so much more.

"Good kitty," he whispers.

I'm still scared—of a whole load of new things now—but I meant what I said. I trust Miller with whatever's to come.

Whether I should or not.

11

MILLER

I seriously didn't want to leave Charlie after all of... well...*that.* But Paul's asked to see me tonight and says it's important. Not urgent, so I consider postponing, but I feel like Bootleg has been neglected enough, and a lot of people are depending on me now.

Still, the blow-up and subsequent conversation with Charlie took a lot out of both of us. And then there was that fucking kiss. Holy shit. I know I've broken every promise to myself, but if we feel the same burning attraction as was made very clear by that earth-shattering kiss, then the rules have changed.

I still have a vow to myself to protect him at all costs. But if he's definitely, honestly not throwing himself at me because he feels like he has to, well...I'm only human. I'm desperate for him like oxygen. I fill my lungs with his scent as we lay curled up together in the spare bedroom. He's so soft against me, and his kisses taste like coconut cream and pineapple.

But it's his big heart that's got me so smitten. He cares so deeply and worries so much. It's crazy that he thinks he couldn't be good enough for me. He already is.

"Charlie?" I say. He's dozing in my arms, and I hate to disturb him. But the sooner I head out to the club, the better. He stirs but doesn't wake. I smile to myself. "Kitten?" I say a little louder.

He blinks his eyes open, his long lashes brushing against his cheeks. My heart clenches. This thing that we've stumbled into might be delicate and somewhat unstable, but I know I'm going to work my arse off to protect it. To protect him.

"I have to go to work for a little bit," I tell him as he surfaces. "I'll be back soon. Do you want to carry on sleeping, or are you hungry?" We had dinner, but I know how after an emotional release, it can often drop the blood sugars, and he might need something.

He yawns and rubs his eyes, coming round further. "I think I'll try and wake up so I can sleep properly tonight," he says sensibly. It's still only early evening, after all. "Um, some food might be nice."

I kiss his temple. "Good kitty for telling me what you need," I say, feeling like this is something I'm going to have to repeat a lot.

Before we can move, a certain little madam stomps over me and then starts rubbing against Charlie, purring loudly. "Aww," Charlie murmurs as he pets her.

"Yeah, yeah," I say to her with an eye roll. "We all know who your favourite is now." She's still mad at me for making him cry, I'm sure.

Charlie laughs, and I watch my two kitties for a minute. I mull his words over about how he wishes he could be more confident, like a cat. It's true. For all they're skittish, cats know what they want, and they take it. They're the queen of the castle. I wonder if there's something I can do to give Charlie some of that kind of confidence.

When Florence has enough and runs off, I take Charlie's hand and lead him down to the kitchen, where I pour him some more pineapple juice (without alcohol this time) and make him some cheese on crackers.

"Feel free to watch TV or use my laptop," I tell him as I gather my things to head out. "If you want to go back to sleep or just snuggle down, I'd really like it if you used my bed. But if it makes you more comfortable, you can stay in your room."

He pauses and swallows the mouthful of juice he just took. "Your bed?" he repeats.

I knew that would trip him up, but I'm done dancing around in a vain effort to protect him. I'm going to be honest with him from now on and ask for what I want. I'm hoping we can get to the point where I just tell him, but I'm still learning his boundaries.

So I nod and move back over to cup his face in my hand, looking into his owlish eyes. "I'd really love to have you stay with me in my room tonight. Just to sleep," I make very clear. "But I want to keep you close. How do you feel about that?"

He stares a second, perhaps considering what to say. "I've never shared a bed with anyone before," he admits, looking away and chewing his lip. Then his gaze returns to mine. "I think I'd like that a lot, though. It sounds nice."

My heart melts, and I lean down to claim a chaste kiss from my little kitten's lips. "I'd like that a *lot*. But if you change your mind, that's okay, too. I might be back late, so I'll just come find you wherever you are, all right?"

"Yes, Miller."

I kind of want him to call me 'sir'. I've been 'sir' for several subs over the years. But it doesn't feel quite right for my sweet kitten, so I leave the matter for now.

Instead, I kiss him goodbye, then order an executive car and make the journey over to Soho.

It's Saturday night, so the whole area is alive with revellers. Even Bootleg is packed, although I'm still dubious about the quality of the clientele. I'll be happier when we clean up and rebrand.

Paul's dressed in the same jeans and a similar polo shirt to yesterday, looking like a kindly uncle. Yet I haven't forgotten the way he dealt with those arseholes last night. I don't think he's someone to be messed around with.

"Evening, boss," he greets me convivially. "Thanks for popping by."

"Sure," I say genuinely. "Is there a problem?"

He shakes his head, which I'm glad of. "No, not a problem. But I wanted to catch you before you really got going with your plans for this place."

I raise my eyebrows. "I take it you have some ideas?"

He nods and looks over the crowd. It's slightly less grubby tonight now that I'm looking. I think there might be a stag do that look to be having a great time and just have a more wholesome vibe towards the dancers on stage.

"I reckon I do," Paul says as he rubs his white beard. "I'm happy we've closed the private rooms. It always made my stomach turn, to be honest. Not the privacy bit the paying for sex. I know it's not legal, and I did my best, but you're right. I couldn't always look out for my boys the way I wanted."

I nod. I suspected that was my father's idea. I'm sure he took advantage of pretty young boys far away from where my mother could hear about it. Or perhaps she knew? Maybe one day I'll ask her.

"Have you informed the dancers yet?" I ask. "I appreciate that was extra income for those taking part, but I'm hoping once the books are straightened out and above board, we'll be able to give them a proper pay rise."

Paul scoffs. "A couple didn't like it. They've already walked off. But between you and me, those were bad apples. I'm not sorry to see them gone. I think we might see quite a change in the atmosphere around here with just a bit of a shake-up."

That's good. I'm all for getting rid of bad apples.

"So what are you thinking?" I prompt him. I don't want to be impatient, but I have a shiny new kitten waiting for me at home, and I'm pretty desperate to wrap my arms around him again and remind myself that he's safe and well and might actually be *mine.*

Paul juts his head towards some of the rooms. I think there are five in total, all varying in size from quite large to around the same as my office. "If we're doing a refurb and a rebrand…what are your feelings on kink?"

I raise my eyebrows in surprise. "I've been thinking about it an awful lot today, actually," I admit. I'm going to need to have a chat with Charlie pretty soon, but he'd had enough today, and I didn't want to overwhelm him. However, it's obvious to me that he's taking to submission like a duck to water, and I want him to fully comprehend what that means and assert his boundaries.

"You in the scene?" he asks, and I nod. "Thought so," he says appreciatively.

I know what he means. I definitely get some kind of Dom vibe from him. We can often feel each other out.

"So here's my two pennies' worth," he continues. "If we're going to shift away from dirty sex club to something nicer, we could make this a kink club instead. Make those rooms into different playrooms. Have bouncers in all of them and different rules on the walls. Keep the boys dancing, and people can tip them if they want, but the rooms will be strictly no exchanging of money and for patrons. Have a clear line between work and play for the boys. If they're on the clock, no playing. But maybe give them special employees' late access or something," he adds with a wink.

I tilt my head and take another look around the place. Suddenly I'm seeing a *really* classy refurb with leather booths, and chandeliers to go with top-of-the-line equipment in these rooms.

I'm seeing it so clearly that I have to remind myself that the plan is to sell it on once it's stable. But I can cross that bridge when I come to it.

"It sounds like you've given this a good deal of thought," I say with a nod. "What about booze, though? We can't have alcohol messing with consent, but drinks sales are what's keeping this place afloat."

"Oh, absolutely not," he says with a frown. "I'm glad you mentioned it. You're a good lad, aren't you?" The 'unlike your father' is left unsaid. "Yup, I was thinking we have wristbands for play. The paper kind you put on tight and have to cut off. You have to have one to get into any of the rooms, and anyone with one can't buy anything hard at the bar. That way we can balance the two kinds of clientele."

I'd want to test it out, but that sounds like a reasonable business model. "I like it," I say. "So you're thinking different levels in the rooms. Public play, impact play, that sort of thing."

"Yup," he says again. "And if you'd consider it, I'd like to put a case forward for a playroom—as in, the kind with actual toys and teddies and a storybook corner."

I blink at him a second, but then he nods over my shoulder.

I look over to see a man probably in his early thirties on a small table by himself, tucked away in a corner by the backstage staff area. When he sees Paul and me looking, he lights up and waves over, then he goes back to his phone, concentrating on something with his tongue poking out.

I look closer at him. He's hugging a stuffed dinosaur, and his T-shirt has Thomas the Tank Engine on it.

Realisation dawns on me. He's a little. He's *Paul's* little.

"You're a Daddy," I say with a nod of respect. I always thought that was a particularly lovely kind of Domineering, although I've not thought much about it myself. I suppose it's not too different from my style, really. Littles have different subspaces, as do middles and boys. Charlie's more a boy than a sub, come to think of it.

Huh.

"I'd love to make this a really *safe* space, boss," Paul says earnestly. "That's what I'd hoped when we opened, but um…"

"My father had a different vibe in mind?" I supply. He nods gratefully.

I hum thoughtfully, Charlie's earnest words coming back to me from earlier. *I feel safer with you than I have with anyone ever in my whole life.*

"Kink should be safe," I say with more conviction. "It should also be freely available and overseen by people who know what the fuck they're doing."

"We could make this a kind of a haven," Paul says with raised eyebrows. "Maybe once a month, we could host demonstrations and such? Those nights could be proper events where we keep it completely sober and open up the whole club."

I rub my jaw. "Thank you for this, Paul. I think it's got real legs. Let's keep fleshing this out next week when everything's shut down."

He puffs out his cheeks in what looks like genuine relief. "Thank you, boss. I mean it. This means a lot to me. I think we could do a lot of good."

I clap his shoulder and bid him goodnight. But as I head

to the door, I'm rolling his words around in my head on a more personal matter. Kink at its best should make you fly. You should feel the safest you possibly can—even if it's part of the kink not to. There are always consent and boundaries in place as well as aftercare. It should be freeing.

Now who do I know who sounds like they could really do with exploring that side of themselves?

I've got some shopping to do.

12

CHARLIE

THE NEXT FEW DAYS GO BY IN A BIT OF A BLUR. THAT SECOND night where I dared to sleep in Miller's bed was only made better when I was woken up by him crawling under the covers and wrapping his arms around me.

I've slept in his bed ever since.

Just sleeping, which worried me to begin with, like maybe he didn't really mean it when he said he fancied me. But the epic make-out sessions we've been having go a long way to allaying those fears. Even if they're only kissing and I've been having to sort out my pent-up needs in every shower.

But when I calm down and think about it, I kind of love that he's keeping true to his word and not rushing me into anything. I've been waiting my whole bloody life, but he seems really concerned about me having a good first time. No—the *best* first time.

I'm just ecstatic to think it might really be with him. He's all but promised me, after all, and there are so many loving things he does that leave me in little doubt of his affections. Like the way he brings me tea every morning and massages my feet and moved all my new clothes into his bedroom in my very own drawer. He's always finding ways to touch me as well. Just small brushes of skin or bumping shoulders. It makes me feel connected in a way I've never experienced with anyone else before.

I'm still me, so naturally, I've still left *some* room to fret. But I'm not sure that can be helped.

I'm feeling better since I've opened up my new bank account. I've even done a shift back at work that was seriously boring, but it made me feel useful. When I approached my manager, it seemed my message the other day was never passed on, but Miller was very firm on not worrying about getting extra time or an advance. In fact, he's hinted a couple of times that it would be perfectly fine to quit this rubbish job and look for something better, but I'll think about that later when things calm down some more.

I'm still reeling from how much my life has changed in under a week, but a lot of it is good change, so I'm trying not to worry too much.

For example, I'm pretty sure I have a boyfriend.

We haven't said the words yet, but that's what it feels like to me. Not that I have anything to compare it to. But we spend a lot of time together, and he cuddles me all the time and calls me 'my kitten'.

My. Urgh, it makes me all squirmy just thinking about it. I've never been anybody's anything before. Mum called me 'darling' a lot, but that was different, obviously.

I really, really like being Miller's kitten. I wish there was a nice name like that I could call him as well. Maybe something will come naturally over time. Meanwhile, I like calling him by his name a lot. Like I'm proving to myself that he's really there.

That he might be 'mine' in return.

I'm able to cook, but Miller is better and has a wider range of recipes, so I tend to feel okay with him doing that.

But I've prided myself on keeping on top of the tidying, loading the dishwasher, and washing up the bigger pans. Especially as he's been in the club a lot the past couple of days, overseeing this big refurb. He really does appear to thrive on taking care of his business as well as me, but I love being useful.

So when he comes home on Tuesday night, I'm just finishing the washing up, and the kitchen is looking spotless, so I've got quite a lot of bouncy energy from feeling proud. Like I've earned my keep just a bit.

"Kitten?" he calls out as he heads up the stairs.

I skip out to the landing on the first floor, then wave like a total dork as he ascends. But he grins and runs up the last couple of steps.

"Hi," he says, touching our noses together.

"Hi," I say breathlessly back.

He kisses me, but it's not supernova like some of them can be. Probably because he's got several pretty pink square bags in his hands. Delicate pink crepe covers the contents. My curiosity is piqued, but I'm more interested in Miller. If he wants to tell me what's in the bags, he will. I trust him.

"Come here, kitten," he says, heading into the living room. He places the bags on the coffee table and sits on the sofa. I'm not sure why, but I feel funny sitting on the sofa with him unless I'm snuggled right next to him. It seems much more natural to put myself on the floor by his feet, so that's what I do.

He lets out a little "oh" noise as he looks down at me. Then he reaches over to caress the side of my jaw.

I raise my eyebrows and second-guess myself. "Should I sit on the couch?"

But he shakes his head. "You're perfect just as you are." My *god,* the praise feels like warm syrup oozing through me. "I actually want to have an important conversation, and it's kind of about this. I'm hoping it'll be a good talk and help you understand some things. I want to ask you a few questions, and I want you to promise to answer me as honestly as you can. Can you do that, kitten?"

I nod eagerly. I want to make him happy, and I trust he won't ask anything nasty or uncomfortable. Or more, it's that I trust that if he asks me something, there will be a reason for it, and it won't be mean or meant to try and trick me. Gio was fond of that, and then he'd laugh at my responses, but Miller won't do that.

"Good boy," he murmurs. "Okay, let's start with...does it feel nice sitting on the floor like that?"

I think before I answer, wanting to give him all the information, even if it's a bit embarrassing. "Um, yes. Really nice. But only because you're on the couch. If you weren't there, I'd probably sit up there by myself." Saying it out loud feels bad, though! "Not that I don't want to be near you!" I squeak.

However, he's already shaking his head and smiling. "No, that's wonderful. Good boy."

I bite my lip and smile as well, squirming a little in relief and happiness. He's moved his hand slightly so he's scritching the short hairs at the back of my head, sending pleasant shivers down my spine.

"And how does it feel when I take charge? Like when I pick out clothes for you or decide what we're going to have for dinner."

I almost don't want to answer. I'm tempted to feel ashamed that he's guessed my secret thoughts. But he's still looking at me like I'm some sort of wonder and gently scratching my neck. So I think maybe it's okay.

"I love it," I say breathlessly, but then I can't stop myself from dropping my gaze to the carpet. "That's probably a bit pathetic, isn't it? I should probably work on that."

"Charlie kitten, please look at me," he says, using that particular tone of voice that goes right to my bloody balls. Urgh, has he guessed that too? I peek up at him. "Do you remember when I told you how happy looking after you makes me?"

"Um, yes," I say. He did tell me that, but I keep forgetting.

"So if you also love when I do that, I'd say that makes us pretty well matched, wouldn't you?"

He brushes his thumb against my cheekbone, waiting for me to respond. I've got a bit fixated on what he just said about us being well matched, though. That sounds an awful lot like he's thinking of us as a couple. A pair.

Eventually, I blink and manage to nod. He sighs happily and just looks at me for a moment.

"Do you know what 'kink' means, little kitten?"

I raise my eyebrows, suddenly worried. "Doesn't that mean you're a pervert?" I say without thinking. That's what I thought it meant when people talked about it at school. If someone did something weird, people would cry 'Oh, kinky!'.

Miller laughs, so hopefully, I've not put my foot completely in it. "I guess to some people it might seem like that," he says with mirth. "It's a sexual inclination outside of what you might call 'vanilla'." He wrinkles his nose. "Some people would say 'normal', but what the hell is 'normal' anyway?"

I hum in agreement. Calling something 'normal' always seems a bit of an insult to me.

Miller goes back to scritching his nails against my scalp. It's a delicious sensation. "Kink often involves a certain power dynamic. But it's very important that everybody involved is consenting, and that's what I want to talk to you about. I don't think you're really aware of how submissive you are or how much you enjoy it, are you, Charlie?"

I blink a couple of times. Am I submissive? I guess. I was

always good at standing up to doctors and pharmacists and stuff to get Mum what she needed. But Miller is right. I'm *much* happier when someone else—when *he*—takes charge of things.

"Am I kinky?" I ask with a frown.

But he just grins. "I think so. But the good news is that I definitely am. What we're doing right now is kinky. You're submitting to me, and I have to say, it's breathtakingly beautiful, kitten."

I feel myself blush as I look away for a second, overwhelmed. He's saying that I'm good at this thing that makes us compatible? Well, then. Maybe I don't fully understand it, but that makes me very happy.

"Kink can literally take you into a different place in your mind, Charlie," he says, getting my attention back. "It's called subspace and it's apparently wonderful. I'd be the one to help you find that inner peace, and that's what makes *me* feel wonderful."

"Okay," I say. I really like the idea of making him feel good like he makes me feel.

He glances at all the bags. I'd forgotten that they were even there. "I've bought you a present, kitten," he says. "It's okay if you don't like it, but I'd like you to at least try it. For me. Do you think you can do that?"

I lick my lips and look the bags over. That's all just one present?

Oh, shit. Are *all* those bags for me? I glance at them, then back to Miller. I can almost feel him daring me to protest, so I let out a shaky breath and remind myself that he literally just said that taking care of me gives him a thrill. That it's part of his kink. And I want to make him happy.

"I'll try, Miller."

He cards his fingers through my hair. "Good boy."

He lets me go then to pick up one of the bags to look

through. He frowns and puts it down, trying another. The crepe paper rustles as he presumably looks at the contents, then he smiles. They're such a nice pink colour. There can't be anything too scary in there, can there?

"Ah. There we go." Then he hands me the bag. "Please open this one first, sweetheart."

I take the bag gingerly.

"Thank you, Miller."

"Good boy."

I push the paper aside and tilt my head, wondering what I'm looking at. There's just one thing inside. It looks black and fluffy. Curious, I carefully remove it from the bag.

It's a pair of cat ears on a horseshoe-shaped headband all covered in soft fake fur.

My stomach swoops. "Are they for me?" I ask hopefully.

He nods. "If you want. You see, there's a certain kind of kink some subs enjoy. They call themselves boys or puppies or kittens, and it's like an alter ego. Or like letting their true selves be free. It can be very empowering and help you to better get into the kind of subspace you might enjoy. It's like giving yourself permission to let go because it's not really you. Or it might be a purer version of you. You'd have to see how you feel. The other night you lamented not really being a cat. But you *can* be, little kitten. My cat."

I gulp, looking between him and the ears. Could it really be that simple? Could I dress up and be Miller's kitten for real? Can I feel the way I do when I'm at his feet like this all the time?

I guess there's only one way to find out.

I slip the headband on with a shy giggle. I feel sort of silly but kind of daring at the same time.

Miller sucks in a small breath, his eyes lighting up. Then he reaches down and adjusts my hair a bit. "Gorgeous," he says.

I'm actually starting to believe him when he says things like that.

He gets me to delve into more of the bags. There are extremely soft, lightweight fingerless gloves with a shape on the palm like the centre of a cat's paw. Fluffy bootie slippers that are designed with little toe beans and claws on the end. Those are both black and pink. Several different comfy-looking cotton shorts with tails attached and more sturdy denim shorts with bigger, more structured tails.

I've already slipped the gloves and slippers on, so with Miller's encouragement, I pick my favourite pair of shorts—a pink pair with the biggest black bushy tail—and quickly swap my jogging bottoms for them. My heart is fluttering in my chest as I look down at myself. He's also got me some adorable T-shirts with cartoon cats on and a funny-shaped harness thing that goes around my shoulders. The tight feeling of having that on makes me feel like he's restraining me almost. Like when he held my wrists in the entrance hallway that first night.

I love it.

There's just one bag left, and I feel like he's been holding it back.

"This one's special," he says, confirming my thoughts as he hands it over. "And when I say you don't have to wear it, I mean it. This isn't just a bit of clothing or an accessory. It means something important."

Frowning, I carefully remove what's inside.

It's a collar.

The black leather is soft and heavy, but there's also a cream fleece lining on the inside that's even softer. A silver tag hangs from the middle with an engraving on it. One side reads: 'Charlie'. The other, in smaller lettering: 'Property of Miller Soldi'.

A sort of keening noise escapes my throat, and my eyes

fill with tears so fast I have to blink them away so I can read the engraving over and over. Miller reaches forwards and catches the wayward tears with his fingers.

"If you agree to wear this, Charlie, you'd be telling the world that you're mine. It's a commitment. Some people consider it like an engagement ring, but I think this could be like a promise ring for us. You'd be promising yourself to me and only me. And you could just wear it here at home, or if you felt bold enough, you could wear it outside to places like Bootleg or at Pride…anywhere that's kink-friendly. So people would know you belong to someone. But like I said, this isn't just an accessory like the rest of the presents I've bought you. So if you need some time to think about it—"

I cut him off by lifting the collar up to him, meeting his anxious gaze with my tearful one.

"Would you put it on me?" I whisper.

He swallows, several emotions playing on his face. I think he might even be a bit tearful as well, and fucking hell, that makes me let out a happy little sob.

He gets down on his knees and sits in front of me before very gently taking the collar from my hands, his fingertips brushing mine. Then I lean forwards as he lifts the collar, sliding it around my neck and fastening it.

I can easily breathe, and he checks the tightness by sliding two, then three fingers under it. But like the harness, it's restricting. As if Miller has wrapped his hand around my throat—not squeezing—just holding.

I'm his.

I belong to him.

I've never been happier in my entire life.

13

MILLER

I watch Charlie as he studies his reflection in the mirror above the fireplace, touching his collar and ears reverently. I'm glad for a moment's respite. I'm still reeling from his complete eagerness to throw himself into the kitten play, but more than anything, the way he was so unafraid to put my collar on.

He's really mine.

I rub my throat, hoping to ease the lump there. No relationship I've ever had before has felt so precious. So important. It's like Charlie needs me to discover who he is, and who he is is *stunning*.

But there's still one thing left to ask him before we can move forward, and I'm apprehensive.

"Kitten?" I say.

He turns and tilts his head to look at me. Am I crazy, but are his shoulders already a little farther back? Is his spine stiffer?

I hope so.

I reach my hand out and beckon him over, which he does

eagerly. He takes my proffered hand and kneels by my feet. I'm sitting on the couch again, so I get to gaze down at him.

That collar stirs something *feral* in me, but I need to concentrate just a little longer and do right by him.

"You know how you like being called kitten?" I begin.

He nods fervently. "I love it," he says breathlessly.

I nod. Good. "Well, there's something you can call me that would make me feel the same, but I understand if it's not a word you like. We can try and think of something different, but you're *my* kitten, and I'd like you to call me something other than my name to show that."

He's nodding again. "Yes, I understand," he says. "I was actually thinking about that the past few days. I'd love it if you had a special name as well."

I exhale, and it's my turn to nod. "A name no one else calls me," I agree. "There's actually a role in the kink community for Doms who take care of boys and kittens, like you. They're Daddies. How would that make you feel? To call me Daddy?"

I've thought about it a lot. 'Sir' was right for those other subs, but it definitely doesn't fit for Charlie, and neither does 'Master'. No. I kept coming back to seeing Paul with his little in the club, and I know that I want to be Charlie kitten's Daddy.

But I honestly don't know how he'll feel about that word, given his history with his own father figures. Lord knows mine isn't simple, either. But my old man was never my *daddy.* He was never nurturing or caring or any of the things I'm desperate to be for Charlie.

"Daddy," he says with a frown, casting his gaze away as he tries the word out. I realise I'm holding my breath. If it's not right, we can brainstorm together to come up with something else, but then he looks back at me. "Daddy and kitten," he says quietly with a nod.

"That's right," I say like he really is a cat and I don't want to spook him. "You're Daddy's baby kitty. Why don't you come here and give Daddy a kiss?"

I figure hearing the word used in context might give him an indication as to whether or not he feels squicky about it. But his eyes go wider, and his chest moves visibly up and down as he starts to pant.

"Yes, Daddy," he says in awe.

My cock practically leaps in my jeans. But that's before he moves from the floor onto the sofa and starts to crawl—fucking *crawl*—down the cushions towards me. Before I can really appreciate what I'm seeing, he's pushing me—Charlie, my scaredy cat, pushing me!—onto my back against the armrest and straddling my hips, rubbing our hard lengths together through our clothes.

"Kitten," I rasp, running my hands up his sides, appreciating how he's looking down at me for the first time. There's a spark in his eyes. It's electric and almost *dangerous*.

And then he pounces.

He seizes my mouth with fierce determination, kissing me with a passion I've never seen in him before.

I fucking love it.

My cock throbs as I jam my hands into his ridiculously thick hair, tugging at it and caressing his brand-new fluffy ears. I keep one hand there as he plunders my mouth, but the other I move down to fondle the collar around his neck.

"Mine," I mumble into his mouth between messy, frantic kisses. *"Mine."*

"Yours, Daddy," he agrees with a whimper, and I could almost shed a tear at the emotion that surges through me.

I think we've both waited long enough. He's desperate, and so am I. It's time to give us both some release, finally.

"Kitten," I say, breaking the kiss and rubbing my thumb roughly over his swollen lower lip. "You *are* Daddy's. And

Daddy wants to know if you've ever been anyone else's. It's okay if you have, but—"

"No," he interrupts me. "No-one, Daddy."

I move my hand from his mouth to cup between his legs, squeezing his bulge. He makes a choking noise as his eyes roll back in his head. "No-one else has ever touched you here?"

I know I'm only stroking my ego, but I don't care.

I need to know if I'm truly the first.

He shakes his head frantically and grips my shirt with fingers that dig into my chest. "No, Daddy. I promise."

I take one of those hands and move it onto my crotch, earning me another delicious whimper from him. "And have you ever touched anyone else here? With your hand or your mouth?"

He's still shaking his head, his eyes glossy and his breathing ragged. "No, Daddy. You're the first. You're the only one."

I growl and drag him back down to kiss me again. "I love that, kitten. That makes Daddy so, so happy. Can you feel how happy he is?"

I rub his hand against my jeans so he can feel just how diamond hard I am for him.

"Yes, Daddy," he cries.

I take my other hand and press my thumb against his mouth, gasping when he sucks me in without pause.

"Good kitty," I tell him. "Do you know what good, sweet kitties get?" He shakes his head, still sucking my thumb filthily. "They get Daddy's cream. Do you want it?"

He stills for a second, staring at me. Then he looks down between us at the point where our groins currently meet.

That's right, little one. That's allll for you.

He pops his mouth off my thumb and takes a few breaths. "I want it so badly, Daddy," he says, sounding hoarse already.

Oh, kitten. *By the time I'm done fucking your throat, we're going to have to come up with some kind of sign language for you.*

I caress the side of his face and the back of his neck. "You can have it, kitten. Enjoy yourself."

For a second, he looks unsure. But I want to see him take the lead on this. I know he can do it.

Sure enough, he starts to reverse back down my body, his luxurious tail swaying from the seat of his booty shorts.

God, he's so bloody edible. I can't wait to taste every single inch of his gorgeous, soft body.

I put one hand behind my head and use the other to play with his hair as he uses trembling fingers to pop the button free on my jeans. "Good boy. Such a good kitty for Daddy," I murmur as he carefully drags the zipper down.

I hiss in pleasure as he reaches through the denim and strokes my length through the cotton of my briefs. He's watching it obsessively, like he's found a lost treasure. Then he fishes inside my underwear and touches the sensitive skin of my rigid cock for the first time.

Oh, *fuck*, that was worth waiting for.

I gasp as he fondles it uncertainly. He looks up, probably worried by the sounds I'm making. So I nod frantically. "That's good, kitten. Great. It feels so nice. You look gorgeous."

He exhales and smiles in relief, then goes back to playing with my dick like it's his new favourite toy.

I bloody *hope* it's his new favourite toy.

I groan as he strokes it and rubs his thumb over the leaking tip, I don't know how, but I'm actually getting harder for him, I'm sure.

And that's before he gives it an experimental lick like it's a lollipop.

"Fuck," I grunt, curling my hand in his hair and making him gasp, his eyes sparkling. Yeah, he likes that. "Good kitty,"

I say again. "Give it a taste. Daddy's got so much cream for you."

He takes a deep breath like he's psyching himself up for it, leans forward, and slips his mouth over the top of my shaft. We both moan, and I run my hand over his hair and fluffy cat ears.

"That's it, kitten," I encourage. I almost remind him to keep his lips wrapped around his teeth, but at least right now, I'm getting off on the little scratches and sharp drags. My kitty has bite.

Besides, there's also the hot suction of his mouth and the way he's rubbing his tongue against my shaft. It's sloppy, but he's gaining confidence, his hesitation fading away as he gets more and more into it.

"Good boy, good boy," I murmur, my chest heaving.

Is it the most sophisticated blow job I've ever had? No. Is it still hella erotic and am I soon about to shoot my load? Abso-fucking-lutely.

This isn't some random hook-up that has to work hard to turn me on. This is my precious kitten, and my heart is aching to see him touch me like this. It was forbidden that first night we met. But there was only so long I could hold back from giving him everything he deserves.

My first blow job was to an older boy at school in a toilet who wouldn't even look me in the eye after he'd come down my throat, let alone speak to me. I felt cheap and nasty.

Charlie is my fucking rock star, and he's going to be left in no doubt that he's bloody perfect.

"I love it, kitten. Just like that," I moan, tugging on his hair. "Touch it with your hands, too. *Fuck*. Yes. That's it!"

With one hand rubbing the base of my shaft, he yanks impatiently at my clothes with the other so he can fondle my balls. They're heavy and throbbing as I rush towards my climax. I thrust just a little into his mouth, adding to all the delicious sensations.

"Charlie," I warn him through gnashing teeth. "Kitten, I'm going to come."

I let go of his head so he isn't forced to swallow my spend. But he stays right where he is, bobbing up and down on my cock with his mouth and wanking the lower half off furiously.

Then I'm arching my back as I begin pulsing, crying out as my vision dances. He coughs and splutters, releasing my dick as I continue to spurt. He gets some on his cheek, but then he dives back on, sucking the tip and draining the last few drops from me.

"Fuck," I gasp.

I cradle his face as he pops off me in a calmer manner this time. He's panting, and his lips are swollen and shiny. I swipe the splash of cum from his cheek with my thumb and rub it against his lips. He sucks the last of my cream down greedily.

"So good," I say reverently. "So very good for your Daddy, kitten."

He beams at me like he's just won a prize.

Little does he know, it's me who's won the best prize of them all.

Him.

14

CHARLIE

I FEEL LIKE I'VE JUST RUN A MARATHON.

With a hard-on.

I'm still balanced on Daddy's thighs, and he's cradling my face with one of his hands as I try and catch my breath. He looks stunningly dishevelled as well, his chest heaving and his cheeks flushed. His wide eyes are locked with mine, our gaze connecting us on some deep, primal level.

What a head rush.

I've thought a *lot* about what sex was going to feel like physically. But it hadn't really occurred to me to think of what it would feel like *emotionally* to be intimate with someone. That was kind of stupid of me, I guess. But I never would have imagined this raw vulnerability running through me, least of all that it would make me feel like I'm flying.

"Charlie," Daddy says in awe.

That's something else I would never have fathomed. I've heard of Daddy kink, I suppose. But again, I thought it was something weird.

It's not, though. It's so *right*. Miller takes care of me like a good parent should in any scenario. I understand why he thought I'd be hesitant to use a word like that but thinking of him as 'Daddy' is like a different part of my mind completely to how I think about my family.

He's my *Daddy* now. It just makes sense.

I'm sort of floating, and I wonder if this was what he meant about getting into a new kind of head space. I feel different as a kitten, but also like he said, almost as if I'm a better, purer version of myself.

This Charlie is less afraid. He trusts his Daddy to know what's right, so he doesn't have to over think or worry about things. Kitten Charlie is sexy and special.

And now he has a belly full of cream.

A nervous giggle rumbles up my throat. I just gave my first blow job. More than that, Daddy seemed to *love* it. His softening cock is right there below me, happy and spent in the thatch of dark curls, lying on his tummy. I can only see a peek of his chiselled abs under his shirt, but he has those lines inside his hips that look like a V, and I trace them both with my fingers.

He laughs like it's ticklish, and I smile shyly at him. "You're so hard," I marvel.

He hums and sits up, wrapping his arms around me so we're cuddling chest to chest. "And you're so soft. A perfect match."

I'm not sure I agree. His stomach is *way* more impressive than mine. But I'm starting to learn that it's okay to just listen to Daddy and trust him. Maybe he really *does* feel like my body is as great as I think his is?

He kisses me lazily, and I melt. I also feel pretty naughty, knowing that he's tasting his own cock on my tongue. Maybe he's right, and I am kinky?

It's funny, because putting on all my kitten gear didn't

seem weird. Neither does calling him 'Daddy'. It feels so natural and right, like I've been searching for this my whole life.

I'll tell you the other thing I'm feeling right now, and that's painfully horny. My poor cock is throbbing, trapped inside my shorts, and pressed up against Daddy's tummy as we make out. I'm gripping his shoulders, and a whimper escapes my throat.

Daddy laughs at me, but it's not unkind. Far from it. I blush at the affection in his eyes as he looks at me so close up. "Little kitty," he rumbles. "What's the matter? Tell Daddy what you need."

"Um, I, um," I say, squirming.

I can't think straight as I rub myself against him, desperate for some friction. He digs his fingers into my back and bites his lip.

"Use your words, kitten," he commands. "Daddy wants to hear you say it."

Fucking hell, my pulse is racing. I'm so shy, but the fact that he's making me say it out loud is dirty and delicious, and it gives me the courage, even if I trip over my words. I don't waver my gaze from his.

"I want...I need...please touch me, Daddy. Down there. I need...to come."

I could almost burst into flames from embarrassment, but I'm proud of myself for saying it.

So is Daddy, apparently.

He captures my mouth for a filthy kiss. "Good boy. Such a good boy. Daddy's going to make you come so hard."

I expect him to reach for the fly on my new shorts, but instead, he gently eases me off his lap before tucking himself away and closing his jeans up again. Then he stands and offers me his hand, which I take to help me on my feet.

Then—*holy shit!* He bends and swoops an arm behind my knees. With the other around my back, he *picks me up.* I shriek and cling to his neck, my heart racing. But once I'm settled in his grasp, I look into his eyes and laugh. It was unexpected, but Daddy is really strong, and I feel safe.

Always so safe.

He nuzzles our noses together and gives me a sweet kiss. Then he hugs me closer to him, and he starts walking out of the living room.

Oh my god, he really carries me all the way up the stairs into his bedroom. I can't help but want to call it *our* bedroom. It's where I'm sleeping, and all my stuff is in there. But that's probably really presumptuous, so I keep the thought to myself for now.

It's not like I'm looking to have a long chat right now anyway. My heart is like a pneumatic drill in my chest as Daddy carefully lays me on top of the bed, my head on the pillows. Then he crawls up behind me, spooning against my back. My fancy new tail is awkwardly between us, but then Daddy hooks his foot over my leg, dragging it away from the other one. My tail is now between his legs, and I'm feeling quite exposed.

I gulp as he starts kissing my neck softly and skimming his hand over my tummy, running his fingers along the hem of my T-shirt. His other arm is pillowed under my head, and I cling to his forearm as he uses his thumb to rub one of my nipples through the shirt. I can't help but shiver and moan, my cock throbbing under my clothes.

"Good boy," Daddy murmurs. "Good kitten, letting Daddy pet your tummy. So pretty."

"Daddy," I mumble as I turn to find his mouth. He kisses me hungrily, his hand slipping under my T-shirt and rubbing all over my skin. *"Daddy."*

It's like a prayer, like a brand-new word that holds magical powers for me. It's not that 'Miller' was wrong. It's his name, after all. But Daddy is who he *is*. It makes me feel like we're so much closer together.

Like he's already inside me.

And oh fuck, this *collar.* I feel it with every breath I take, reminding me of what it says and what it means. The insecurities rattling around my head are strong, but how can they compete when Daddy has literally made a claim on me that anyone can see?

"Daddy, please," I whine, bumping my nose against his cheek.

He chuckles softly. "Yes, kitten?" he asks innocently. "What was it you wanted?"

I don't know where it comes from, but I'm blaming the collar. And everything else he bought me, but I feel like it's the collar that drums up the little growl from my throat as I pout and glower at him for being a tease. Then I grab his hand from under my T-shirt and slap it right on top of my straining erection inside my shorts.

He drops his head back and roars in delight. I only get a second to grin in pleasure before he's seized my mouth again, kissing me roughly. "Sassy kitty," he mumbles against my lips.

I'm half-laughing, half-groaning as he manages to deftly undo the shorts with one hand and yank both them and my underwear down my thighs. My cock springs out, and I gasp as air hits the wet tip, but then his hand wraps around almost the whole length, squeezing tightly, and I whimper and thrash in his arms.

He holds me tighter.

"Who does this belong to?" he asks, squeezing my shaft.

"Daddy," I cry.

He licks and nibbles at the shell of my ear. "And who do you belong to?"

"Daddy, Daddy," I say more urgently.

He sucks my earlobe into his mouth, which would make me shiver anyway. But he also starts stroking my length, and I feel like I'm going to vibrate out of my skin.

"That's right. Just Daddy. Only Daddy. No one else, ever."

I shake my head frantically in agreement.

"Daddy, please, Daddy," I babble. I squirm against him and thrust into his hand. The headband, collar, and harness all dig into my skin. Daddy moves his other hand and restrains both of my arms against my chest.

I feel surrounded and trapped, but in the best possible way. I don't want to go anywhere. I just want to be Daddy's. I want him to do whatever he wants with me. I'm at his mercy, and it's the safest feeling in the world.

His hand flies over my cock, which is now slippery with precum and jerking wildly against his palm. "Have you got some cream for Daddy?" he rasps, nuzzling against the side of my head and then biting my earlobe. The little *zing* of pain goes straight to my balls, and I cry out in shock and pleasure. "You like that, don't you? So good. So needy. Come on, little kitten. Come for Daddy. Give me all your delicious cream."

I screw my eyes shut, and suddenly it's like I can feel just how restrained I am by him. He's my whole world. I'm pinned down like a mouse under a cat's paw. I wail, my climax crashing over me like a tidal wave. I don't think I've ever shot such long ropes of cum. They spurt all over my body, hitting my skin and my new clothes. He's still tugging mercilessly, wringing every last drop from me as I howl and moan, thrashing in his grip.

Then it's like the needle drops and I hit empty in an instant. I flop against him, and I don't know why, but I burst into tears.

Before I can get embarrassed, Daddy is there. He manages to turn me without crushing my tail, and then he's hugging me fiercely and pressing kisses all over my tear-stained face. He doesn't seem to care that I've lost my mind or that my mess is smearing all over his clothes. He just keeps kissing me and rubbing my back, his limbs wrapped around my whole boneless body.

"Good boy, Charlie," I realise he's saying. "Such a good, pretty little kitten for Daddy. So perfect. I'm so proud of you." I take deep gulps of air, pressing our temples together and blinking for a while. He repeats those soothing words until I feel like I come back to myself.

Whoa. That was kind of intense.

"Daddy?" I croak.

"I'm right here, beautiful. How do you feel?"

I feel achy and sticky, but I'm quite sure that's not what he means.

How do I feel within myself?

The shock after I orgasmed was…well…a shock. I didn't expect such a rush of emotions, and, I guess, adrenaline and endorphins as well. But now I'm breathing steadily, and I know I'm safe in Daddy's arms. I can feel my fingers and toes tingling. My heart might still be beating fast, but it's light, like a hummingbird in my chest.

And my mind…it feels like it's had a wonderful shower. Like it's been rinsed out with minty bubbles.

"Good," I finally manage to say. Then I lick my lips and shake my head. "Amazing," I correct myself. "Oh, fuck. Daddy."

He keeps hugging me, but he moves his head so we're kissing again. This time it's slower, less frantic. But there's still a heat there that makes my heart sing. *"You* were amazing," he mumbles into my mouth. "I'm so proud of you, little kitten."

I had no idea you could make someone proud by having sex. But I don't care. If Daddy says he's proud of me, I'll take it and run.

Except I'm not going anywhere.

I belong in his arms now.

15

MILLER

It's like I'm living in a dream. My house has become a bubble that's protected from the rest of the world. It's just me and Charlie in our little fantasy land.

The week that follows is a strange mixture. On the one hand, I'm working at the now-closed Bootleg, overseeing the refurbishment, meeting with my accountant to go over the bar's books, and making decisions on paint samples and which kinky equipment best blends style, safety, and price.

On the other hand, I'm just Daddy, and my little kitten is waiting for me whenever I get home. He wears the clothes I bought him on the first day when he leaves the house, but as soon as he's back inside, it's nothing but ears and tails and those adorable paw slippers. I've already washed things for him several times, but if he's this enthusiastic, I'm going to look into expanding his wardrobe sooner rather than later.

My favourite thing, though, is that he's now got a pretty ceramic bowl by the front door. He removes his collar when he goes to work or if he pops to the shops, but then he puts it back on the second he walks through the door, before he even takes his shoes off. The best times are when I can be there to do it for him.

Again, I'm already considering if I can get him something smaller and symbolic that he can wear in public. I think he misses the feel of it against his neck when he has to remove it, so there's got to be a pretty choker I can find for him as a stand-in.

It's as I'm searching online for this very item with him curled up asleep on the couch beside me that the sudden thought strikes me.

Have I lost my mind?

Seriously. It's the weekend again, so it's been just over a week since we met. Eight days. And it's felt completely natural to turn my whole life upside down for a guy who walked into my life offering to sell himself to the highest bidder.

That makes me crinkle my nose in disgust. Thinking about Charlie in that way feels like a different dimension. Another lifetime. He's mine now. *Mine.* He's under my protection, and his fuck-up of a stepfather can't hurt him anymore.

But am I moving too fast? Am I truly being responsible here? Charlie is young and excitable, throwing himself into not only his first relationship but his first taste of kink as well. There's no doubt in my mind that he's a sub and that he's taken to his kitten role exceptionally well. I know that it's good for him.

But has he just accepted me as his Daddy because I was the first to come along and offer that option to him?

Fuck. It's not like me to be insecure. Not since I got away from the house I shared with my father and brothers, anyway. But I've never fallen for someone so quickly, let alone absorbed them so completely into my life. There's a horrible voice at the back of my mind (that sounds an awful lot like my late father) that's telling me that Charlie's just using me for my money, my house, and all that. But…I offered him those things freely.

More than that, as I look down at his face, even more innocent in sleep, I try and search for anything that might indicate his affections are anything less than sincere. I can't. We may have both fought this at the start because we were clinging to ridiculous notions. But Charlie wears his heart on his sleeve.

No. The problem is me. I'm not used to anything so pure and good in my life, and I think there's a part of me that's *looking* for a reason not to trust it. To protect myself before it comes back to bite me in the arse. As if Charlie could ever betray me.

My father trusted no one because he was convinced everyone was out to stab him in the back. Probably because that's what he did to everyone. That's how he got so filthy rich. I tried not to be like that, but I think some of it has rubbed off on me anyway. It certainly has on my brothers. They're just as ruthless and ambitious as he ever was, and now they're running his empires with even more power than they had before.

They'd probably mock me mercilessly if they knew about Charlie.

But have I really been any better than them with my heartlessness? Yes, I've used some of my talents to help Mother run her charities, but I've mostly used the money that was given to me to swoop in and buy up failing companies, then sell them on once they were fixed, not really caring if they got broken up or what happened to the employees. I was also pretty blasé with my past relationships. I think I figured if I could keep those men at arm's length, I'd protect myself from getting hurt the way my father and brothers used to hurt me.

But then I inherited Bootleg the same day I met Charlie, and I don't think that's a coincidence.

Because there's a small part of my brain now that's whispering that I don't have to do things just because that's the way it's always been. Bootleg isn't just some bar. It might have been my father's dirty little secret, but that hasn't stopped it from turning into something special in spite of him under Paul's tender care.

It's a family.

One that I wouldn't mind being a part of. Lord knows my own family leaves a lot to be desired.

It's like Charlie's brought a ray of sunshine into my life. Scratch that. He's the whole bloody sun. And I'm starting to believe things could change.

Am I a fool, though? Is this just the endorphins of a shiny new relationship? Is my thrill at introducing him to sex and kink life giving me rose-tinted glasses?

Can I really be in love after just a week with a kitten almost half my age?

Maybe I shouldn't be making any big life decisions now, like what I'm going to do with the bar. Everything's in too much flux. I've gone from someone who could take or leave kink before to a full-time Daddy. And just because right now it feels like bliss, it doesn't mean that everything won't come crashing down eventually.

I bite my lip and close my laptop, turning to gently stroke Charlie's hair. His security has got to be my priority as well. I've made a commitment by putting that damn collar on him. I have to put his needs first, no matter what.

Even if I realise that what's best for him is *not* being with me.

There's no reason to think that other than a lifetime of cautiousness. Still, it tugs at my heart. I wish I could feel more certain that something isn't going to tear down this new life of mine simply because it's not as cold and detached as the one I was living before.

After all, isn't that why all my other relationships failed? My exes said as much. They felt like I was too distant, like I always had one foot out of the door.

And yet here I am, buckling up a collar around this young boy's neck after only knowing him for a couple of days.

I'm sure most, if not all, of my exes would keel over in shock if they knew.

But perhaps I'm giving my father and brothers too much credit in judging my own character. Just because they're alike doesn't mean I have to be. Mother might not have been all baking cupcakes and finger-painting with me, but she absolutely loves me. I'm even thinking about mentioning Charlie to her in our next weekly video call.

I am capable of loving and being loved, no matter what the rest of my family have tried to convince me.

I can *choose* a different life. I can choose to be happier and kinder and more considerate of others. Perhaps Charlie came into my life at just the right time?

Perhaps he was meant to save me?

He stirs against me. "Daddy?" he mumbles before he's even got his eyes fully open.

I beam down at him. "Hey, kitten. You fell asleep. Do you want to go up to bed?"

"I want to stay where you are," he says, his eyelids already drooping again.

My heart melts in my chest.

Why do I have to be so cynical and second-guess everything? Why do I have to look a gift horse in the mouth? *Two* of them. Charlie and Bootleg. Perhaps this is just the start of the next chapter in my life. A better one.

"Well, I'm ready for bed, so let's move up there," I tell my beautiful kitten. "Come on. Daddy's got you."

I leave my laptop in the living room. Any emails can wait until the morning. I used to be glued to work twenty-four seven. But none of that seems as important anymore.

Not compared to the gorgeous young man I scoop up into my arms.

"Time for bed," I tell him with a kiss to the cheek.

"Okay, Daddy," he says happily, nuzzling his face against my chest with his arms around my neck.

I get him changed and help him brush his teeth before getting him into bed because that's what I do now. I take care of everything for him. It's my joy, my privilege.

And there's no reason to think that has to stop any time soon so long as I don't get in my own blasted way.

16

CHARLIE

My nerves are threatening to shred me up worse than a cat on a curtain. But I'm holding my ground. I've got nothing to be scared of. Daddy knows best. So if he doesn't think this is a good idea, he'll tell me, and I'm sure he'll be kind about it.

I feel sick at the thought of his rejection, though. My mind keeps spinning out of control, thinking that just by asking for this, he's going to be disappointed in me or disgusted with me or…oh, I don't know what.

My insecurities have been better this past week and a half, but still, I'm not going to undo years of abuse from my stepdad that fast. I can't stop myself from imagining scenarios where Daddy finally realises I'm no good after all and kicks me out.

In one of my more logical moments, I mustered the courage to come up with this plan, and now I'm sitting on Daddy's bed, surrounded by rose petals and candles in my favourite kitten gear, trying not to completely freak myself out.

He's due home any minute. I just need to breathe.

I close my eyes and stroke my own luscious tail, loving

the soft, tickly fluff. I would never have dreamed in a million years of trying on these things, let alone that when I did, I'd feel them transform me. They're just clothes and accessories, after all. How can they have such power over me?

But they do.

Charlie might be nervous, but kitten isn't. Kitten Charlie knows what he wants, and he's going to pounce.

Daddy put money in my new account, so I don't have to ask him for every little thing I need. I've directed the shop to pay my next wages in there as well. It feels good to be a little independent, even if I love Daddy taking care of everything most of the time. I needed my own money to surprise him today, for example.

I swallow and take another deep breath, smiling as I think of the rose petals that I've scattered all the way from the front door and up both flights of stairs to the bedroom. They're not from actual bouquets—that would be crazy money—but a bag of biodegradable flower petals online was only a few quid, surprisingly. And I found the bag of tealights in the kitchen.

Besides, as worried as I am about being frugal still, I know that Daddy is worth both the money and the effort. Surely, he won't be mad that I made a mess.

Right?

I guess I'm about to find out.

I hear the front door opening from all the way up on the top floor. I hold my breath, gnawing at my lip as I strain to analyse any tiny sound I can discern. Was that a chuckle? Is that a good sign?

Daddy's footsteps sound unhurried as he makes his way through the house. I think he pauses in the kitchen and gets a glass of water. My heart is racing so loudly now I'm struggling to make out any other noises. Oh, *fuck*. This was a crazy idea. Daddy's the one who's supposed to take charge and make decisions! I don't even like doing that! I know I wanted to surprise him, but what if I've misjudged and got it all wrong? I should run and hide in the bathroom right now and get changed. I should—

"Hello, kitten," Daddy's low, rumbly voice cuts through my frantic thoughts. I was so preoccupied that I didn't even see him come and stand in the doorway.

The sight of him takes my breath away.

He might have just come from meetings and the hustle and heat of London in summer, but he looks cool and fresh in his shirt and jeans. The top buttons are undone, so I can glimpse a little peek of chest hair.

But none of that matters. Not really.

It's the way he's smiling at me that makes my heart rate finally start to calm. It's lazy, like he's got absolutely nowhere else in the world that he'd rather be. And the little crinkles around his eyes are more pronounced as his mirth reaches them. His whole expression practically smoulders, sending tingles down my spine. He toys with one of his thumbnails like he's trying to give off an aura of calm, but the way he licks his lips as he stares at me says otherwise.

"Hi, Daddy," I say breathlessly, suddenly nervous for a whole different reason.

I'm pretty sure I'm about to get *ravaged.*

"You've been a busy little kitty, haven't you?" he says, his voice warm with amusement. "What a lovely surprise for Daddy to come home to. Is there a special occasion?"

I wince. Damn it. Would it have been more romantic to wait for our two-week anniversary? I've never celebrated anniversaries before. Well, there's no going back now.

"You're the special occasion," I say coyly, my heart hammering in my chest again. He could still say no. He might not think it's time. "I'm, um, ready for you."

I wish I didn't sound so hesitant. It might have been

better if I'd waited for him to decide when the time was right. But I really *do* want to do something special for him. And absolutely not in a repayment manner. I think I'm finally past that now. I just want to try and spoil him a little after the way he's spoiled me *so* much.

His eyebrows rise, and he comes into the room, standing by the bed in front of me. "You're ready?" he repeats as he caresses the side of my jaw, making me shiver. "For me?"

"Yes, Daddy," I rasp, hoping he understands what I mean.

The past few days have been incredible. I've had more hand jobs and given more blow jobs than in…well… obviously my whole life. But also more than I've had hot meals. It's been exquisite. Daddy loves feeding his kitten his cream and milking kitty's cream from him.

But I'm ready for more.

I'm sure I am.

That's why I spent the past hour using one of Daddy's toys that I found on myself. I cleaned it thoroughly before and after, so I really hope he won't mind. Especially when he realises I'm all stretched and waiting for him.

Ready for his cock.

I'm ready to lose my virginity…if he's willing.

His mouth pops open, and he takes a couple of breaths as his gaze travels over me. I'm not wearing a T-shirt under my harness like usual. I'm a bit self-conscious of my tummy, as I'm not at all ripped like Daddy is. But he's said over and over that he loves my soft belly, so I decided to be brave.

I'm rewarded as he skims the back of his knuckles along the top of my shoulder, then down my chest to brush one of my nipples. I gasp and bite my lip, already quivering in anticipation.

"What are you asking Daddy for, baby kitty? Use your words and be very clear."

Oh, lord. I'm already blushing. I can't quite look him in the eye. "I w-want you to be my first, Daddy."

He touches his thumb to my chin and gently tilts my head so I have to look him in the eye. I pant and try not to squirm. "The first to what, kitten?"

He's going to make me spell it out, isn't he? I guess full, enthusiastic consent is important, but I'm on the verge of a panic attack at having to articulate such an intimate request out loud, especially whilst Daddy is looking into my eyes like he can see my very soul.

"I want…the first…" I'm not sure I can do it. But then Daddy leans down and gently kisses my mouth. My eyes flutter closed, and I exhale. "I want you to be the first to fuck me," I murmur against his lips. "I want to give you my virginity. I trust you, Daddy."

"Oh, kitten," he says like he's in awe of me.

I open my eyes and look into his beautiful blue ones. He carefully touches the collar around my neck that's become like a second skin to me. He rubs against the edge as he studies me like I'm rare and precious.

"I don't understand what I've done right in this life to deserve you, but I don't have the words to adequately say how grateful I am. You are beautiful inside and out, and I'm so lucky you're mine."

I try and swallow the lump that's risen in my throat with just a few short sentences. "Daddy," is all I can whisper.

I've been reading up on kitten play. Apparently, the more I embrace my feline alter ego, the deeper into subspace I can fall. Part of that is moving away from speech and trusting physical action. So I do my best not to overthink it as I nudge and butt my head against his stomach, softly vibrating my tongue against my front teeth so it sounds like a real purr. I've been practising that for days, and I think it sounds good. But when Daddy gasps, I think I've done it right.

Then I meow.

I thought I'd feel stupid, but it's oddly freeing. I do it again as I look up at him, trying to convey how earnest I am with just my face. I also rock my bum from side to side, making the tail on my booty shorts swish. Daddy's watching me, his mouth agape. But rather than feel stupid, my confidence grows. So I rise up on my knees and place my paws on his chest, angling my fingers so my nails point down against his shirt like claws. I can feel them pressing against his skin, and his heart is thundering under my palm.

I tilt my head, our gazes locked together, then let out another little mewl.

He seizes my face and crashes his mouth onto mine, kissing me like a drowning man gasping for air. His tongue plunges into my mouth, and he moans as he pushes us back onto the bed—sideways so as not to damage my lovely tail.

I grab his shirt and whimper as he plunders my mouth and manhandles my body. "Kitten. Oh, kitten," he growls against my lips.

Okay.

I don't think I fucked this up. In fact, I think I've gauged this just right.

17

CHARLIE

I THINK THE REASON DADDY RUSHES TO GET MY SHORTS OFF first is to protect my pretty tail. But maybe he also guessed that I was already naked underneath them.

He groans as he crawls on top of me, kissing my lips roughly and rubbing his denim-clad thigh against my erection. He also pins my hands above my head, which he hasn't done before, and it sends a delicious thrill shivering all over my body as he holds me down and snogs my face off.

"Kitten," he mumbles into my mouth. "Baby kitty. Daddy wants you so badly. My pretty kitty. So good for Daddy. So perfect."

He's kind of babbling, but I fucking love it. I'm doing that. I'm making this cool, older man who has his shit completely together in life become a frantic, horny mess.

Technically, I'm still a virgin, and I'm already driving him this wild. What the hell? Is it going to get better than this?

In a horrible flash, I worry that Daddy's only this excited because he's about to take my V-card.

Is he going to lose interest after this?

I suddenly feel sick.

"Charlie?" he says in concern. *Shit.* I realise I've gone all still and weird on him.

"I'm fine," I mumble, trying to convince both of us, but it doesn't work.

"Charlie," he says again with a frown. "Sweetheart, what's wrong? If this isn't what you want, we'll stop right now."

I shake my head. "It was my idea," I protest.

He frowns in disapproval. "That's completely irrelevant. You say stop, we stop. Even if I'm literally about to come. Are you safe wording out?"

"What? No!" I blurt out.

I wriggle, and he immediately sits up, giving me room to do the same. He holds my hand and caresses the side of my face. My cock is losing some of its hardness, and I feel small. How did this happen so fast?

"I'm being stupid and ruining everything," I utter in shame.

He does that thing where he tilts my head and makes me look at him. "Talk to me," he commands. "Be honest. What happened? You were so excited. Did I do something wrong?"

"No!" I cry, feeling more ashamed and upset. "It's my own stupid insecurities. I'm sorry. We can just forget it."

"Charlie," he says in a warning tone. We've had a chat about kinky stuff, and I said I'm not particularly interested in being punished for being bad in a fun, sexy way. But in that moment, I know who's in charge, and I need to obey him because I care about him a lot. Besides, Daddy knows best.

But I don't want to accuse him of feeling something he probably never felt. Or...of confirming my fear.

"Charlie, you're worrying me. Tell me what it is right now."

I gulp, unable to look at him, especially with tears in my eyes. I blink and turn my head.

"Are you this excited because it's my virginity? Will it not be as special another time? Will you...not want another time?"

He lets out a huge breath and grabs me into a fierce hug. "Oh, kitten," he says in distress. "Thank you so much for telling Daddy. I'm proud of you. Thank you. But you've got nothing to worry about. I'm excited because my gorgeous boy left a trail of rose petals through my house and then was a very sexy kitten begging me to have sex. I'm thrilled to be your first. I'll take such good care of you. But it's only going to get *better* after this. I promise. And yes, there will be many, *many* more times to come."

I concentrate on breathing in and out for a while, processing his words. I can't believe how fast I spiralled out of control, but that fear was real. I think because I've placed such a high value on my virginity—I literally tried to sell it for crying out loud—I've got some idea in my head that it was all I'm worth.

Of course Daddy is able to help me see that's not true.

"I spoiled the mood," I say after a while. I let out a sad little laugh. "I'm sorry."

Daddy scoffs, then leans back to look into my eyes. "You haven't spoiled a single thing, kitten. In fact, you being honest with me makes it even better because I can do my best to allay any of your worries and make you happier. That's my whole job as your Daddy."

"Surely, it would be better if I wasn't so insecure to begin with," I say, rolling my eyes.

Daddy shrugs. "I love taking care of you, Charlie kitten. It makes me feel good, remember? There will be plenty of other times when we make love when you feel confident, and I'll enjoy them all, I know. But this time will always be special, and part of that will be the fact that you were brave enough to check in with me."

I wouldn't phrase it like that. I'd say I freaked out and

cockblocked myself. But maybe Daddy's right, and it was good this happened now. If I hadn't said anything, I'm sure I would have wondered if my suspicions were right. Would have worried.

Besides, it's only cockblocking if I don't get any, and no one's taken that off the table yet.

"You make everything so special, Daddy," I whisper as I look into his eyes. "I'm glad you like the petals."

He gives a soft, easy laugh. "I *love* them. No one's ever done anything like that for me before."

"Really?" I say with raised eyebrows. I haven't asked about any of his exes. I don't particularly want to know. But it's kind of awesome to think little ol' innocent me managed to do something none of them ever did.

Daddy smiles, but—*oh*—there's heat to it again. "Really," he murmurs as he cups his hand behind my head and leans me back on top of the mattress. He kisses along my jaw. "I like all the candles, too. So romantic. Perfect for my pretty kitty. Although, you've kind of put me to shame. *I* should do things like this for *you*."

I giggle. "I'll let you most of the time, Daddy, I promise. But we can romance each other, can't we?"

He shakes his head faintly as he looks down at me. Like he can't quite believe what he's seeing or hearing.

I get that feeling quite a lot when I'm with him.

"You can romance me any time you like, kitten," he says as he kisses my neck. "But now it's Daddy's turn to take care of you, all right?"

"Yes, Daddy," I say with a happy sigh.

I regret that I had such a wobble, but I don't regret Daddy making me be honest with him. I'm extremely glad I heard his earnest answer.

He likes me for me. In fact, I think he likes me quite a *lot*.

I whimper as he presses his fully clothed body down on

my mostly naked one. I've still got my booties and fingerless gloves on, so it creates interesting sensations as he smothers me, claiming me with his mouth.

"What's your colour, baby kitten?" he murmurs against my skin. We've talked about the traffic light system before, but this is the first chance we're really getting to use it.

"Green," I say truthfully. I'm starting to feel floaty already, like I do when he cuddles me and wanks me off, whispering sweet nothings in my ear about how good and pretty I am.

He kisses my jaw and sucks on my earlobe. "Tell Daddy what you want."

"Kitten wants Daddy deep inside," I say, realising that it's easier if I do what he does and talk about myself in the third person. I'm not embarrassed as I grind my thickening, exposed cock against his hip. "Kitten wants Daddy to take his virginity and be his first. What does Daddy want?"

He blinks and looks momentarily surprised by the question, but then that warm fondness returns to his face like he's utterly delighted by me.

I'm really starting to believe that's true.

"Daddy wants to make kitten the happiest he can be, always," is his answer.

My heart feels like it's going to burst.

I recall what he said just a minute ago about not knowing how he got so lucky. I feel exactly the same way. It was such a strange series of events that brought us together, but I can't help but think that's the way it was supposed to be.

There's an aching within me that I'm not quite sure how to describe. I only know that I feel complete when I'm with my Daddy. There's a deep sense of peace for me in his home. It's like we're already connected and he's not even inside me yet.

It's amazing, and if I could stop getting in my own way,

I'm pretty sure it's a feeling that's only going to keep growing.

Speaking of personal growth, I've got some going on both metaphorically *and* physically. My cock is back to being extremely hard and excited, but my confidence is blossoming again like a flower in my chest. I tug impatiently at Daddy's shirt.

"Off," I command with a pout.

He drops his head back and roars with laughter. "God, I *love* sassy kitty," he says with a grin as he looks back down at me.

My heart skips a beat. Did he just say the L-word? No. He said he loves when I'm bossy, not that he loves *me.* Two different things. It's fine. It's way too early to be saying things like that anyway. I shake it off and grin too as I hastily help him unbutton his shirt and push it over his shoulders.

"These as well?" he teases me, hooking his thumbs under the waistband of his jeans.

"Yes, Daddy," I huff impatiently. *"Everything* off, please."

"Bratty baby," he says fondly as he kisses me filthily, thrusting his tongue into my mouth and biting my lower lip. "Are you hungry for Daddy's cream again?"

"Yes, but in my arse this time," I say naughtily, earning another raucous laugh from him.

"Anything for my kitty," he growls, unbuckling his belt and sliding it through the loops on his jeans.

I've already got my hands on his button and fly, unzipping him so we can both push the denim down. Except he grabs his briefs as well, and suddenly he's completely naked with me for the first time. I'm familiar with his cock— I've sucked him off several times. But seeing it standing proud now, straining from the thatch of thick hair between his solid thighs and under his muscular torso, I'm struck by how much of a *man* he is. His musk is deliciously masculine as well, and I love how nice and hairy his hard body is.

He's everything I dreamed of in my lonely teenage years and more.

And now he's all mine.

He runs his hand through my unruly hair. It's always annoyed me how thick it is, but Daddy loves it, so I'm starting to appreciate it more. Then he fondles one of my cat ears, which obviously I can't feel, but I can sense the pressure of the band moving against my head, so it still sends shivers down my spine.

Neither of us even hints at me taking my kitten gear off so I'm naked as well. I know without having to vocalise it that would feel wrong. Kitten is who I am. My accessories make me feel strong and bold, just like a real cat. Their touch against my hot, damp skin gives me power.

So much so that I purr again and lightly headbutt Daddy's chin, meowing and batting at his side. His look is pure molten as he looms above me.

"Are you ready for me, kitten?" he rasps. I nod. He shifts and moves his hand between my legs, rubbing over my hole and making me gasp. "How ready?"

I blush, but I don't chicken out. "I was a naughty kitty," I whisper, holding his gaze. "I stole Daddy's toy and stretched myself so I'd be nice and wide for Daddy's fat cock."

I swear I see his eyes dilate right there and then. He breathes heavily as he brings his hand back around and pushes two fingers against my mouth. I swallow them down hungrily, licking them like a lollipop. When they're wet enough, he removes them and goes straight back to my hole, pressing them against my entrance. I groan as they slide in with relative ease.

"Oh, *fuck*, baby kitty," he gasps.

Without wasting any more time, he scrambles off me and

yanks open the bedside cabinet on the side that he sleeps. I noticed a couple of days ago there was lube and a box of condoms in there. He gets one of the shiny foil wrappers out as well as the new bottle, popping the cap off and drizzling a good amount onto his hand.

He crawls back to me and doesn't hesitate to ease three digits into me this time. I feel the difference—it's been a while since I had the dildo up me now—but it's still okay. I did a thorough job earlier.

"Oh, kitten," Daddy says, shaking his head as he pulses his hand slowly, making me moan and writhe. "You're so perfect. You were right—you are all ready for me down there. Do you feel ready in here?"

He uses his other hand to tap my heart, which contracts with such affection for his kindness I almost don't know what to do with myself. I *am* ready, though, so I manage to nod.

"Please, Daddy," I beg.

He doesn't mess around.

He gently withdraws his fingers and wipes them on the duvet cover. Then he grabs the condom packet to rip it open with his teeth. *Urgh*—that's so fucking sexy, especially because he keeps eye contact with me the whole time.

I watch as he rolls it down his rock-hard cock, then squeezes more lube along it and also around my crack. He wipes his hands off again, and then he's positioning himself above me, cradling the back of my neck and holding my collar with one hand. With the other, he's lining himself up, rubbing the tip of his length against my fluttering hole.

"Who's going to take care of you?" he asks, his voice heavy and his eyes practically black with desire.

"Daddy," I say so earnestly it almost brings tears to my eyes. "Daddy. Only Daddy."

"Good boy," he murmurs as he kisses me softly. "Daddy's kitty."

I gasp as he pushes inside me. Despite all my preparation and experience with toys (I had a couple hidden away at home, too) it's still so different to have a hot, hard cock pushing past my tight ring of muscle. Even though I want it so badly, my body is still fighting the intrusion just a little. It's such an alien sensation.

"That's it, beautiful," he urges me as he pushes in a bit farther. "Just breathe. You're doing so well for Daddy. You feel amazing."

I close my eyes and press my temple against his, inhaling and exhaling steadily. It's tight, and it kind of burns, but it's also incredible. The fullness is all-consuming and I feel completely claimed by my Daddy. I grip onto his back, pulling him closer, like that will draw him inside me as far as possible.

I thought I felt connected before, but I was right in speculating that this would be even more. It's unreal. Like we're just one being now, fused together in passion and awe.

"Daddy," I whimper as he fills me all the way to the hilt and clings to me, too. "Oh, Daddy."

"Good kitty," he praises me, kissing me all over my face. "You feel incredible. You're doing so well." He gives his hips a little thrust like he's testing the waters. "How's that?"

I let out a gasp that's almost a sob. It's so strange and intrusive but it's also dazzling and perfect. I'm overwhelmed thinking I almost gave this moment away to whatever sleaze had the highest offer.

This is something monumental between me and my Daddy, and no matter what happens next, I know I'll treasure it for the rest of my life.

"Good," I cry, my chest shaking. "So good, Daddy. I love it."

He does it again, rolling his hips and watching me so closely that our noses are practically touching. "Do you like that?" he rasps, something primal and almost dangerous in his voice. It sends a thrill rushing through my body, but I know I'm as safe as I could possibly be.

I also know I'm his. I surrender myself to him completely to own and control. Daddy's in charge, and it's fucking *bliss.*

"I love it." I really do sob this time as he keeps on thrusting. He hits my prostate, which I've been able to find with my toys before, but holy *fuck,* that doesn't compare in the slightest to a red-hot man fucking me with his throbbing cock.

I wail, holding on for dear life as he starts to set a pace. I dig my fingers even more into his back to keep up. He gasps, and for a split second, I think I've done something wrong. But then he's nuzzling our noses together and panting, his cock sliding in and out of me in long, powerful strokes.

"Scratch me, kitten," Daddy growls, that primal undertone in his voice growing stronger. "Mark me with your claws."

My heart hammers in my chest as I do what he says. I change the shape of my hands, so my nails start digging into his flesh, dragging them along his shoulder blades as he pummels me into the mattress.

"That's it. Fucking *yes,*" he cries as our pace gets more frantic. Because I'm not lying there like some pillow princess. I'm thrusting my hips just as hard, meeting him blow for blow. He's slamming against my prostate now, and stars are exploding in front of my eyes.

I had a vision of this lasting ages, but in this moment, I know both of us are chasing our release. There's a frantic rawness as we rut like animals, like all the pent-up sexual tension since we first laid eyes on each other is finally being set free.

It would be so easy to lie there and take it. That's what I want after all, isn't it? For Daddy to take charge. But the kitten in me is clawing his way to the surface and taking over. The whimpers that escape my throat become meows and hisses. God, it's like I'm a desperate beast in heat, feral for my mate to push me all the way over the edge.

I give him one last scratch along his flanks, as deep as I can. It makes him throw his head back and snarl, the tendons in his neck straining as he grunts and thrusts. But then my kitten finally takes over and pushes him—hard. I use my knees and hips to roll us to the side, then suddenly I'm the one straddling *him.*

He blinks in shock for a second, then reaches up to grab my head, hauling me down for an open-mouthed kiss filled with lust and desperation. "Oh, *kitten,*" he moans. "Good kitty. Daddy loves it. Ride his big fat cock and come all over him. Good boy. *Good* kitten."

I dig my fingers into his chest as I ride him. This time it's me who throws his head back as his cock hits inside me at a deeper angle that I love. I bounce and grind, squeezing my knees against his chest to anchor myself. I want to fuck his brains out. I'm overwhelmed with how much I...

With how much I love him.

I'm too far gone to corral my thoughts into something more sensible. All I know is that feeling of wholeness and safety and rightness has grown tenfold. My heart races, and I'm pouring with sweat. Daddy's skin is flushed, and I can see the little welts from my nails already plumping up on his chest. The room stinks of masculinity, and the air is filled with our grunts and cries and the slapping of skin. I look down at my man in disbelief, his features dancing in the flickering candlelight.

I think this might be heaven.

Then he reaches between us and starts wanking me off

frantically. I shriek and mewl, thrashing my head as I slam myself down on him over and over. "Come for me, pretty kitty," Daddy says, his voice strained and hoarse. "Show me just how beautiful you are."

It only takes a few more seconds before I'm doing what he says. Thick white ropes start painting all along his body as I shake. My balls pulse like they're spasming. I don't think I've ever come so hard in my life, but what makes it better is that even through the condom, I can feel Daddy's cock throbbing as he spills inside me.

It seems like minutes, but it's probably only seconds until we're both gasping for air, our bodies going limp. I crash down on top of him despite the mess I've just made. I don't think Daddy cares because he hugs me so tightly to him that he almost squeezes the air out of my lungs.

"Daddy," I mumble as I shake. "Oh, Daddy."

"Good boy," he says as he clings to me. "So good for Daddy. So beautiful. How do you feel?"

Sore. I can't help but chuckle. My hole is tender, and all my muscles feel like I've spent the day moving furniture around or something. But I know that's not what he means, and I don't want to worry him.

"Incredible," I manage to say, holding off the giggling fit. I'm awash with adrenaline, and it's obviously making me giddy. But as I start to come back down, I cling tighter to my Daddy, using his solid form to ground me. "Oh, fuck. That was perfect. Better than perfect. Better than I ever imagined."

He cups his hands on either side of my face, capturing my mouth for a sweet, sentimental kiss. It's not scorching like before, but there's still a hot possession to it that stirs the blood in my veins, even though I've literally only just come.

I wanted my first time to be special, and it was. Unbelievably so. But I think Daddy's right.

It's only going to get better from here on out.

18

MILLER

"THIS IS DAMNED GOOD CRAFTSMANSHIP, BOSS," PAUL SAYS AS we look around one of Bootleg's side rooms that's currently under construction. There are a couple of guys working on installing weightbearing hooks into the ceiling and putting together one of the racks that I ordered.

I nod as I look around. Paul helped make most of the decisions with me. He's been in the scene for years and knows his way around all the ins and outs. I had to be honest and admit that I've not played much in clubs. I mostly just liked to be bossy in the bedroom at home.

Now, though…

I'm looking at our playroom and thinking of a certain little kitten. Would my Charlie enjoy something like this? Pet play has undoubtedly brought out a scrumptious side in him that I would never have predicted. He's like a bird uncaged, stretching his wings and flying free for the first time in his life.

Our first time together was mind-blowing. He worried me for a minute, but our conversation—although slightly painful—was important and illuminating. I'm growing closer and closer to him every day, and it feels like such a privilege. I can't wait to make love to him again very soon.

He's bringing out something new in my life, too. I always thought markings were a subby trait, but I fucking love being scratched up by him. His collar is my way of claiming him, but those welts feel like his way of claiming me right back. It's wild.

"Daddy, Daddy!"

We turn to see Paul's little—Eric—bounding up to us, clapping his hands. I'm not sure if he has a job, but every time I'm here overseeing the refurbishment with Paul, he's here as well, excitably helping where he can and giving enthusiastic praise for all the changes.

"Baby boy," Paul says affectionately. He's never not delighted to see him, and it's beautiful to witness. Paul cups the side of Eric's face as Eric dances on his toes. "What is it?"

"Come see the day-care," he says, grabbing Paul's hand and tugging it.

That's the name we've settled on for the age playroom, and it's been quite charming designing it—not to mention extremely different to all the decisions I've been working on for the other rooms. One day it's spanking benches and chains, the next it's teddy bears and building blocks.

I smile as I follow Paul and his little into the room. Eric hums and skips over to the wall where a big rainbow mural is drying. "It's so pretty! But you can't touch it because it's still wet. And there's this new rug, too!"

He drops to the floor on top of the large rug that looks like a cartoon town map and grabs a toy car from a nearby bucket full of them. He makes adorable 'zoom' noises as he drives the car along the images of the streets.

Paul beams and kneels down beside him, murmuring softly so I can't hear, but the love between them is palpable. The crack of his knees was very audible, however, and I'm glad I've ordered a couple of plush armchairs for the Daddies who will want to sit and watch their boys play in comfort.

It's such a sweet scene.

It makes the intrusion even more awful.

"What the ever-loving *fuck* is going on here?"

I spin around so fast I almost give myself whiplash. I'd know that voice anywhere, not to mention that mocking tone.

It belongs to the person who's bullied me my whole life.

"Gilbert," I grind out, doing my best not to clench my fists. "This is a safe space. Kindly get the fuck out."

My oldest brother scoffs and shakes his head down at Eric, who's shrinking against Paul. "It's a grown man making 'brum brum' noises in a nursery. So *this* is what you've been wasting your time on whilst the rest of us are trying to keep the family business at the top of the Fortune 500."

I grab his arm as he continues to chuckle, marching him back out into the main body of the club. There are plenty of tradespeople working in here as well, though, so I continue to steer him onwards to my office. My heart contracts as I hear the distinct sound of Eric's sniffles, but I channel that pang of sympathy into my fury.

"What the fuck are you doing here?" I demand as I slam the door closed behind us. "This is my business. Haven't you got a textile factory in India full of children you need to be exploiting?"

He's not ruffled, though. Of course he isn't. He just laughs my barb off. "Oh, come on now, brother. You know we haven't done that since the nineties."

He gives me an exaggerated wink that makes me sick to my stomach. I know Father's wealth helped me get massively ahead in life, but I've never been more glad that I've always worked independently of him and distanced myself from all his human rights violations.

Including working on the kinky club that Dad might have seen as a dirty secret, but I already hold so much dearer than that.

"My business is none of your business," I say coldly. "You weren't invited. So I ask again—what the fuck are you doing here?"

He shrugs and looks around the office that I haven't got around to personalising yet. He must see as much of our father in here as I do from the art on the walls all the way down to the choice of colour for the carpet.

My urge to take a flamethrower to it and start again from scratch just increased by a hundred percent.

"I was curious," Gil says with a malicious smile. "I assumed you'd do the sensible thing and sell this money pit on immediately, but here I see you're buying the highest-quality sex swings and settling down to story time with mentally disturbed deviants."

Guilt tugs at me. The plan always *was* to sell it. But lately, I've been wondering more and more if that's what I really want. I'm building something I care about here. Something new and fresh and close to my heart.

"You're really going to throw stones?" I snap, sidestepping his accusations.

I used to be afraid to fight back with him, but when I grew up and found my independence, it felt better to stand my ground. He can't hurt me anymore. Not in any way that matters.

He rolls his eyes. "It's a sex club," he scoffs. "A *gay* one that you're apparently indulging. I think I can throw whatever stones I want."

"What happens here is *honest.*"

Or it will be now, I add mentally. It wasn't the way Father did it. But that's the whole problem, isn't it? Father was so ashamed of his sexuality that he hid it away and made it grubby. But worse than that, he took every opportunity to spout homophobic shit and ridiculed me mercilessly when it became clear that was the way I leaned. Naturally, Gil and our other brother, Victor, copied him.

"Honest?" Gil repeats back with a laugh. "It's mentally unstable. God, if the tabloids discovered what you're up to—"

That's a threat.

I don't like being threatened.

"And what if the tabloids found out about the barely legal girl you're fucking?" I snarl. "Never mind that. What would your wife and *kids* do if they knew?"

I hate the kind of person I become when he goads me. I'd never hurt my nieces, and my sister-in-law is a pretty decent person for a lawyer. But I'm not afraid to go for the hypothetical low blow if it gets my brother to back off from Bootleg.

It's not just me he's threatening, after all. It's Paul and Eric. It's all the young dancers and other staff working here.

He narrows his eyes, not finding all this as funny anymore.

"This nonsense you're indulging in is bad for the reputation of both the family and business," he says coldly. "Billions of pounds are at stake. Thousands of jobs."

Of course he cares more about the money than the people. In fact, I'd wager that he only added that last part to try and tug on my heart strings. Tough. He's bluffing. It's *his* reputation he cares about. He's worried his gay little brother might embarrass *him.* He doesn't want to be uninvited from the best clubs or left off the most important guest lists.

"Everything here is legal and above board," I say because I've made bloody sure it is now. "If it's not to your personal taste, then I simply suggest you never come back." I gesture towards the door.

But he doesn't move, at least not in that direction. He

does fold his arms across his chest and give me a nasty smirk. "I'm not the only one who's fucking someone barely legal, am I, brother?"

My blood runs cold. Of course he's had me investigated. It's second nature to him, just like it was with our father. Dig up dirt on the enemy and then use it against them.

"I don't know what you're talking about," I say coolly. After all, he's talking shit. Charlie is twenty-one and perfectly legal. In fact, the consent has been both enthusiastic and very, very frequent.

Gil continues smirking, though. "That little boy toy you've hidden away in your house. How much are you paying him to be your sex slave?"

I can't help it. He's touched a nerve, and my temper flares. It's probably because of how I met Charlie and his insecurities that I was using him as a fetish or his misplaced notion that payment had to be involved in some form if we were going to be intimate.

I jab my finger in Gil's face, seeing red. "He's a sex *kitten* who *meows* when I fuck him," I gloat savagely. "It's the best sex I've ever had—the kind you'll never know because you're such a selfish prick you never care about anybody but yourself. I bet you need a fucking *diagram* to find the clit."

Infuriatingly, though, he still looks smug, the bastard. "Ah, but you *are* paying him, aren't you?"

Heat creeps up my neck. I'm not getting into this with him. I refuse.

"I take *care* of him," I say. "And he—just like this club—are none of your fucking business. So sod off, why don't you?"

Gil shakes his head. "I run this family, now," he says, his tone dangerously low. "I will do whatever it takes to protect it. You'd really jeopardise that for this little whore?"

I'd have slugged him for calling Charlie that, but I see the bigger picture immediately.

He's threatening Charlie.

"My boyfriend has nothing to do with you or your business," I say, doing my utmost not to tremble. I can't show him how afraid I am.

But Gil tilts his head. "You'd honestly choose that child over your family? The business that made you a millionaire?" He laughs cruelly and throws his hand up to indicate the club. "Hell, over this dump? You always were a poor businessman. Where are your priorities, brother?"

"With him," I say without hesitation.

Don't get me wrong. I'll fight tooth and nail for Bootleg and all my new employees. But Charlie has become my world. It doesn't matter that it happened fast. It only matters that it's real.

Gil laughs, but this time in disbelief. "Really?"

"Yes, really," I snap. "So don't you fuck with him. Don't fuck with me or my business, either. I'm warning you, Gilbert."

He raises his eyebrows, completely unamused. "Or you'll what?" he asks softly.

I swallow. He knows I'd never really drag his name through the mud. I wouldn't do that to my nieces. And his wife might not care about the affair—*affairs.* Hell, she probably already knows. She's a savvy woman.

I don't really have any power here, and I detest it.

As the moment drags on, Gil's smile grows sharklike. "That's what I thought." He turns towards the door finally, but not before looking over his shoulder back at me. "I've made my opinions clear, little brother. It's up to you to decide what you do next. To decide what's right for the family."

I'm left to quiver in rage as he lets himself out the door, whistling a jaunty tune as he heads towards the exit.

One thing's for sure. I'll do anything to protect Charlie. I just don't know exactly what that is. I screw my eyes shut and grit my teeth.

Is it selling the bar after all?

Is it leaving him?

I feel my heart threaten to break clean in two at the mere thought of it, but my brother is ruthless. He could drum up false charges and get both of us thrown in prison if he wanted. He could truly ruin our lives.

I have no doubt he knows a bloke who knows a bloke who could *end* them if he really wanted to take it that far.

I'm sure I could weather any storm, but Charlie's been through enough. I have to protect him.

Even if it means destroying my own happiness.

My temper flares for the second time that evening, and I lash out and slam my fist against the desk, making its contents jump.

"Fuck!" I bellow.

What the hell am I going to do?

19

CHARLIE

I'M PLAYING AN ADORABLE GAME OF FETCH WITH FLORENCE IN the living room when the doorbell rings. I pause, and so does she, both of us looking at the stairs that lead down to the entrance hall. I've never heard the doorbell ring aside from when we've ordered takeaway, but I certainly haven't done that. When it's just me, I make a simpler dinner. Daddy's the one who takes charge and orders food if we fancy it.

My heart leaps. What if he's ordered something before he left work? It could be a surprise. "Let's go find out!" I whisper to Florence as I jump to my feet.

She rushes down the stairs with me. Having hesitated, I don't want to keep the delivery person waiting. But when I yank the front door open and see the imposing man in the suit, I freeze.

He's definitely not got any pizza.

"Charlie?" he says, his voice as smooth as velvet.

My blood runs cold.

How the fuck does he know my name?

It doesn't help that Florence dashes under the chest of drawers and hisses. I glance down at her, then back at the stranger. He's probably a foot taller than me with broad shoulders and a chiselled jaw. He's smiling at me, but it doesn't quite meet his eyes. Eyes that look oddly familiar…

I pull the door closer and stand in the gap. It's silly to think I could block someone like him from getting in, but my hackles are raised, and I'm feeling protective of Daddy's home.

"Do I know you?" I ask with raised eyebrows.

I swear his gaze drops to my collar, but it happens so fast I can't really be sure. Luckily, that's all I'm wearing of my kitten gear today.

"No," he says with an easy laugh. "But I believe you know my brother well. I'm Gilbert. He's spoken so fondly about you."

Shame washes through me. I'm treating the poor man like a criminal, and he's Daddy's *brother.*

"I'm *so* sorry," I splutter, stepping back and indicating that he's more than welcome to come in. It doesn't matter that Daddy's never really talked about his brothers. I know he has two, and he's obviously spoken to Gilbert about me if he knows my name. "Come in, please. D-Miller isn't here, but he should be home in a bit."

Gilbert smiles. It still doesn't really reach his eyes, but some people are shy, aren't they? "Thank you. That's very kind of you."

He scrubs his shiny black shoes on the mat and closes the door behind him. There's an uneasy pause.

"Um," I say. "Like I mentioned, Miller is at work, but he's due home in a little while. Did you want to wait? Does he know you're coming?"

Gilbert gives me a lopsided smile. "'Home,'" he muses, and a prickle rushes over my skin.

It *is* Daddy's home, but I guess I'm talking about it like it's mine as well. I am living here, so that's not too presumptuous, is it?

"I'll wait," he carries on, looking around like he hasn't seen the place in a while. I wonder how close he and Daddy really are. "Shall we sojourn to the living room?"

I'm not sure what that word means, but I figure he wants to head to the lounge, and that will be better than hanging around awkwardly in the entrance hall, so I lead him up there.

I notice that Florence stays under the chest of drawers.

"Would you like something to drink?" I offer as he sits down. He unbuttons his suit jacket and flops onto one of the sofas, spreading his legs and taking up all the space. I notice he hasn't taken his shoes off, and I feel too shy to ask him to.

"No thanks," he says with that same bland smile.

His eyes are trained on me, and it's making me feel a little uncomfortable. I'm tempted to hide away until Daddy comes home, but that would be rude. So I sit on the corner of an armchair and clasp my hands together, wishing I'd got some water for myself. My mouth is dry.

"So, Charlie," he says convivially. "You live here now as I understand it?"

"Um, yeah." I look down and realise that Florence has reappeared. She's purring loudly as she winds her way around my legs over and over. It's silly, but I feel less alone now she's here.

"Because you're Miller's boyfriend?" Gilbert prompts.

I'm feeling really uneasy now, even with Florence there with me. I lick my lips and weigh up the question. It's innocent enough, isn't it?

"Yes," I say simply. We've not actually discussed that label. He's my Daddy. But I definitely don't feel okay saying that to Gilbert, so boyfriend will do for now.

He leans forwards, his hands threaded together between

his knees. He tilts his head and assesses me. "And how much is he paying you to let him fuck you, little boy?"

My breath catches in my throat. It's like I've been slapped. "I...that's not..." I splutter. But Gilbert doesn't seem that interested in listening to me.

"My brother's not the smartest one in the family," he says with a dark chuckle. "He never was very good at spotting a gold digger. But I can see you very clearly before me in that ridiculous collar of yours."

My hand shakes as it flies to my throat. What the hell is happening?

"Miller has responsibilities," Gilbert says, his smile finally fading away. I think it was probably fake all along. "To his family. To our business. I don't know what perverted ideas you're putting into his head." He looks me up and down, his disgust clear. "I can only assume you're spectacular at sucking cock and it's addling his weak mind. But I am not weak. I will not stand for some little freak with pound signs in his eyes dragging my brother's name into the mud. If the tabloids find out about what's going on here, it could destroy the whole family. Not to mention the business and the thousands of jobs it provides. This underage kinky fuckery is absolutely unacceptable. He always was a fudge packer, but at least he kept it quiet and civilised."

Something in me snaps. How *dare* he talk about my Daddy like that.

"He's a good man!" I cry, jumping to my feet and clenching my fists. Florence hisses again from under the armchair. "I'm not a child or a gold digger or any of those other things. I'm Miller's boyfriend, and I *love* him."

It just falls out of my mouth. I've known it's true ever since we made love a couple of nights ago, but I haven't been brave enough to say it to him yet. I hate that I've said it to his bullying homophobic brother first, but now's not the time to be splitting hairs. I've got bigger problems.

I let Giovanni terrorise me because he held all the power over me and Mum. But Daddy's given me my own power now, and I don't just mean financially.

I don't know if he loves me back, but he certainly thinks the world of me and has taught me to start loving myself after only a couple of weeks.

He's made me stronger. Strong enough to stand my ground against this arsehole.

"We're not doing anything wrong. We're two consenting adults. I'm sorry if you don't like it, but that sounds like a you problem. So kindly get out of Miller's house. Now."

He doesn't move, though. And if anything, he appears amused by my outburst.

"I have no idea what goes on in this twisted little house or that filthy club of my brother's, but I'm giving the orders now, kitten."

Anger flares inside me. He doesn't get to call me that.

Except, I guess he does.

"Frankly, I couldn't give a good god damn what you think," he continues. "My family is in a state of flux after my father's death. Our enemies are on the hunt for any weakness they can exploit." He clicks his fingers and points at me. "A dirty stain such as yourself could be used to ruin our business. Is that what you want? To destroy the man you supposedly love?"

All the air rushes from my lungs. No, *no!* I don't want that at all. I owe Daddy so much. I'd do anything for him!

Gilbert smirks, probably guessing my thoughts from my face. "Oh, yes. Miller could lose everything. His businesses, this house, his inheritance. All because of one little kinky slut who's sullying his reputation. So here's how it's going to go, kitten. I will write you a cheque—see? I'm not a monster.

And you'll leave. Tonight. Once you're gone, my brother will see sense and rid himself of that dive bar. My father gave it to him as a joke, but he seems to seriously be considering running the place, and I *can't* have that." He spreads his hands and smiles at me again, but this time I can clearly see it's all bullshit. "This doesn't need to be a big problem. Not when the solution is so simple."

I've broken out in a sweat. Leave Daddy? Right now? *No, no, no!* That will kill me.

But what if what Gilbert is saying is true? If I stay, I could cost him everything. Leave him with nothing.

Just like Giovanni did to me.

I could never do that to someone else, let alone Daddy. I try really hard to hold it in, but a little sob escapes my chest. I don't want to leave Daddy, but I can't hurt him either.

Whilst I've been warring with myself, Gilbert has produced a chequebook and is signing it with a flourish. "Cash that or don't," he says with a shrug as he rips it off and leaves it on the table. "But you will leave this house now under my supervision. I'm a busy man, so I'm giving you fifteen minutes to pack your things, and then we're out of here. I'll drive you to a hotel where I've got you a room for the night, and then you're on your own." He flashes me a smile that's positively vicious. "Cats are known for fending for themselves, aren't they?"

I swallow down my grief. I want to talk to Daddy. He'll know what to do. But...I guess I can do what Gilbert says now, then sort this out later. As he stands from the sofa, I'm reminded of how very large he is. He could drag me out of here if he wanted to. What's the worst that could happen? I'll go to the hotel, then come back when I've spoken to Daddy.

"Okay," I whisper.

He smirks and picks up the cheque, holding it out to me. "I knew money would be your priority. Clever boy. Maybe this way my brother will make it through this transition with his assets and reputation intact." He raises his eyebrows as I close my fingers around the cheque, not letting it go. "I will be watching, kitten. And listening. So you won't be crawling back into his bed. You'll take this money, find someone else to con into fucking you, and never, ever darken this door again. Is that understood?"

I look up at him, trembling. He'll be monitoring Daddy's house? His *phone?* That kind of scuppers my whole plan.

Oh, god. I don't have a choice, do I? If I want to save Daddy, I'm going to have to do what his brother says. My chest tightens, and I feel sick, but I nod.

"What was that?" Gilbert asks with a crooked eyebrow, tightening his fingers on the cheque.

"I understand," I whisper.

He lets it go, and I stare at the bit of paper, feeling hollow. I don't want his money, but it's for *thousands* of pounds. More than enough for me to stay somewhere until I find a house share and get a better job.

I can't help but blink back tears as I look around the living room. But I want to stay *here.*

"Fifteen minutes," Gilbert says, tapping his watch which probably costs five times the amount written on the cheque I'm currently clutching. "I don't know how many lives you've used up already, kitten, but I'm giving you a bonus one back. Do not squander it."

I nod meekly again, then hurry from the room to head upstairs.

I can't stop the tears from falling as soon as I'm alone. Big, messy sobs rack my chest as I stumble into Daddy's room and begin opening drawers. I try not to think too much beyond packing. But acid washes in my stomach as I look at all the lovely presents Daddy bought me.

I don't feel right taking them.

So I move away from the clothes and just empty my toiletries from the bathroom. Those aren't personal. Neither is my phone charger. I put them all in one of the fancy square bags from when we went shopping, along with the clothes that I arrived at his house in. They look so shabby compared to everything else. But they're clean, and they're really mine. I also take some underwear for practicalities' sake.

I feel bad keeping the clothes I'm wearing, but I don't want to keep Gilbert waiting any longer than necessary. However, a fresh wave of grief washes over me as I touch my neatly folded jeans and chinos, T-shirts and button-downs. All gorgeous. All mine. Or at least they were.

But then I open my kitten drawer and just dissolve.

This was who I became with Daddy. I blossomed. I loved being his kitten. But I can't have that anymore.

I'm just about to slam the drawer shut when I give in, taking the black pair of fluffy ears as a memento.

It's less than five minutes before I'm back downstairs, and Gil looks impressed. "Good," he says, sounding satisfied from where he's sat back down on the couch. He puts his phone away, then slaps his knees as he stands. "Shall we?"

A piercing yawl splits the air as Florence headbutts me— hard. She does it again, trying to trip me up as she entwines around my legs. "I'm sorry, baby girl," I whisper, tears flowing down my cheeks again as I reach for her. "I have to go."

She swipes at me, drawing blood from four long scratches across the back of my hand. I inhale sharply at the pain, and she hisses at me.

Gilbert rolls his eyes. "We're leaving, boy," he says, marching out of the living room.

My last look at Florence is of her sitting on the floor, her tail swishing angrily back and forth.

I bite my lip and make myself stop crying as I follow

Gilbert down the stairs. As we get to the front door, he looks pointedly at me. "I assume you have a key?"

I blink. Oh, of course I have a key. And he wants me to leave it here. I fish my set out of the bowl and go to remove mine. But why do I need my old house keys anymore either? They don't work. Gio changed the locks. And the glittery cat keyring that Daddy gave me just makes me want to sob again.

So I drop the whole bunch back down again.

Then I look at the other empty bowl and realise there's something else I need to leave.

It's a good job I feel numb as I place my bag on the floor and raise my trembling hands to my collar. Otherwise, I'd collapse into a heap and howl. But I'm not allowed to be Daddy's kitten anymore. I'll only hurt him if I do. Maybe ruin him.

I should be furious at Gilbert as my fingers fumble with the clasp, but I only feel empty. As I drop the collar into its bowl for the last time, it strikes me it's like I never even lived here. It's as if the last few weeks were just a blip.

Maybe Daddy will forget about me. I just hope he sees the sense that Gilbert is talking and won't hate me.

I realise as we close the front door behind us that I guess I'll never know.

20

MILLER

I'M IN A FOUL MOOD FOR THE REST OF THE EVENING. I TRIED to keep my thunderclouds to myself, but Paul wasn't afraid to turn his Dom side on me. I can't blame him after the way my brother upset Eric, so I told him everything. How Gil was threatening to ruin not just me but also the club and, most importantly, Charlie, unless I do what he says and toe the line.

Paul was sympathetic but—in my opinion—foolishly optimistic. He reckoned Gil was just having a tantrum because he personally finds me and my lifestyle objectionable, but that he can't really do anything truly malicious.

Despite working for my father, it seems he doesn't really know my family all that well.

Eventually, he at least convinces me that I'm no good at Bootleg and should just head home. I don't want to be shirking my responsibilities, but he assures me he has it all in hand and I should get out of his hair. In the end, I partly agree because I want him to stop dealing with me and instead tend to his little boy, who is still clearly upset by what my fuckwit of a brother said.

The other reason I agree is that selfishly, I just want to forget all about this for a few hours and lose myself in my beautiful kitten, even if that's just holding him whilst he sleeps.

I'm bone-tired as I exit my car and head up the couple of steps to my front door. But my heart soars as I slide my key into the door, knowing that Charlie is on the other side, and that means I'm home.

When I step inside and close the door, I'm greeted by my cat wailing from up the stairs like the world is about to end.

Then I look down and see Charlie's collar in his bowl and wonder if it really has.

His keys are also there, and fear immediately crawls up my throat. He wouldn't leave without his keys, so why is his collar off? He removes it to shower, but he leaves it in the bathroom and puts it right back on when he's done.

"Charlie?" I bellow as I run up the stairs without removing my shoes. Florence is still howling, and I see her cross the landing from the kitchen to the living room. "Charlie? Where are you?"

He's not in either of those rooms, so I rush up to my bedroom. He's not there either, but a quick glance in the en suite tells me his toothbrush is gone. His charger isn't by the bed either. But his clothes are still in the drawers. What the hell is going on?

Realisation hits me.

My brother is *just* like our father. He always gets what he wants, no matter what.

My heart is a lump in my throat as I jab my finger against his number on my phone, then wait for the call to connect. I rest my hand on the tail of Charlie's favourite pair of shorts. He's left all his kitten gear, and that's killing me almost as much as the collar. Has he really rejected everything I gave him, including his kink?

The call connects and I don't bother with any niceties. "Where is he, Gilbert?" I snap.

He chuckles. "I see you've made it home. The words you're looking for are 'thank you, brother'. I did what I knew you wouldn't. What you *couldn't.*"

Dizziness rushes over me, and I grab the edge of the chest of drawers for support. "Have you hurt him?" I rasp.

Gil scoffs. "Don't be so dramatic," he chastises me. "He's fine. I gave him a pretty penny and set him up for the night, so he left of his own accord. I don't know what you thought you had there, but I told you. He's just a whore who happily took my money and left you without a second thought."

My heart flips in my chest. "You're lying," I growl.

Gil laughs maddeningly. "I'm just looking out for you, brother. I *saved* you from that pervy little gold digger. I told you he was going to ruin you, but you wouldn't listen."

"No, *you* threatened to ruin him if I didn't do what you say," I say. I don't trust a word he's saying. In fact, I have nothing left to say to him.

Well, maybe one more thing.

"I warned you to stay away from him," I snarl with all the fury I'm feeling in my chest. "I'm going to find him, and then I'm going to *destroy* you for daring to go near him. You hear me?"

Gil laughs again. "If you say so, brother."

The line goes dead.

I squeeze the phone in my hand. He's no brother of mine.

Before I can smash the mobile into the wall, I take a breath and try calling Charlie. As soon as I hear his voice, I know everything will be okay.

It goes straight to voicemail.

It's fine. He could be underground. I force myself to stay

calm and head downstairs, where I finally pour the stiff drink I've wanted to knock back ever since that arsehole waltzed uninvited into my club. Ten minutes go by and then twenty, and the call still isn't going through.

Has he blocked me? No. I wouldn't be getting his voicemail if he had. But knowing that isn't getting me any closer to talking to him.

I scrub my face in despair as the second tumbler of Scotch swirls in my veins. Could my brother be right? Could Charlie really have had a price high enough that he was willing to walk away from me without a second thought?

No. No, when we first met, we almost imploded because we didn't communicate properly. I'm not going to assume anything. I'm going to track him down and *talk* to him. I'll believe he never really loved me if I hear it from his own lips.

Maybe.

Because I'm sure he loves me or was at least falling in love.

I know I was.

Am. I *am* in love with him. It felt too soon to say it out loud, but I've known it for a while. I love him like crazy, and I'm not letting my brother tear that down without a fight.

After half an hour, I give up on his phone and try a different option. I call Paul's mobile, as he's probably still at the club. "Yeah, boss?" he answers on the third ring.

I exhale in relief and pinch the bridge of my nose. "Paul, thank god. Is Charlie there?"

There's a pause, and my heart sinks. "No, mate. Haven't seen him since that first night. Even then, I only caught a glimpse, but I'd remember that hair. Why do you think he'd be here?"

I take a moment to rein in my temper before answering. "I'm pretty certain that my brother came here and manipulated him into leaving."

"Came to your house?" Paul clarifies, clearly outraged on my behalf. It makes me feel the tiniest bit better.

"He said he paid Charlie off and that Charlie was only too happy to take the money and leave, but—"

"Nope," Paul says. "Sorry, boss, but I don't believe a word. Not from what you've said about the boy. There's more to it, I'm sure. Is there anywhere else he could have gone?"

I shrug helplessly, even though there's no one here but my cat to see it. "He wouldn't have gone home. His stepdad changed the locks. He doesn't have any other close friends…"

I trail off.

I'm going about this the wrong way. I shouldn't be thinking of where Charlie might go.

I should be thinking of where *Gilbert* might take him.

"I've got an idea, Paul," I say as I hurry back down both flights of stairs. Florence has stopped wailing, but she certainly does her best to trip me up as she runs alongside me. "I'd appreciate it if you keep an eye out for him as long as you're at the club, just in case. But I think I know where he might have gone."

Paul agrees, wishes me luck, then closes the call. As soon as I lower the phone from my ear, Florence screams at me again.

"I know, I know," I plead with her as I race to the front door. "But it wasn't my fault this time, I swear." I mean, it sort of is if I take responsibility for being related to a complete wanker, but he's pretty dead to me now. "I'm going to bring him back. I won't come home until I find him." She sits on the bottom stair and glowers at me as if to say, 'you better'. "Don't worry, baby girl. I'm just as determined to get him back as you are."

Just in case Charlie comes home on his own, I take a moment to slide his key off his bunch so it will lie flat. Then I put it under the outside mat before locking the door with my own key and jogging down to the street.

My brother's arrogance isn't just a business asset. It's a weakness. He didn't care back at the club that I knew all about his affair, but maybe he should have cared that I know exactly where he always meets this girl. It's where he's met every girl he shouldn't have been sleeping with, and one time when a board member got in some serious trouble a while back with drugs and prostitutes, where did Gil stash him?

Bingo.

I don't waste time calling my usual car service. I just hail an Uber that's only a few minutes away. I'm betting my entire inheritance that Gil sent Charlie to his favourite hotel. My heart thumps in my chest for the entire drive like it's trying to burst through my ribcage. "It's okay, kitten," I murmur to myself as I watch the London streets pass by in the dark. "I'm coming. Just hold on."

It feels like it takes forever to navigate the route there, but finally, we pull up, and I'm giving the driver five stars and a tip before I even get through the front doors to the lobby. It's not the fanciest of hotels. I guess the point is to keep a low profile. But it's not shabby either with its tiled floors and bouquets of fresh flowers. It's certainly quiet at this time of night with no one else around. The reception is still staffed, though. I imagine Gil would have picked somewhere that is staffed twenty-four seven for obvious reasons.

"I've got a booking for Soldi," I bluff as I approach the front desk with a nod. "I believe my friend might have already checked in."

The receptionist narrows her eyes at me. "You're not Mr Soldi," she says.

Fair enough. They probably have strict privacy policies here too. I reach for my wallet. I don't want to throw around the 'do you know who I am?' card, but I will if I have to.

"No, but I'm his brother," I say, showing her my driver's licence. "He made the booking for me and I'm meeting my *friend* here." I emphasise 'friend' in case making her think it's a clandestine rendezvous helps. Sure enough, she gives me a smirk.

"I see, sir. Very well. Here's your key."

She doesn't get me to sign anything, confirming my suspicions that Gil planned all this out in advance. I should have thought to come to this hotel as soon as he said he'd 'sorted Charlie out for the night', but at least I'm here now.

"Thank you," I say, already hurrying away from the desk. I take the elevator up three floors, then rush quietly along the hallway, counting the numbers under my breath until I reach the correct door.

I pause outside it and catch my breath. It's not like I've been running, but my heart is pounding, and my lungs are tight from worry and stress. I want to be composed for Charlie, though, and I'm shaking a bit with adrenaline from the hope that he's just the other side of this door.

I don't want to startle him, so I knock. "Charlie?" I call out softly through the wood. "It's me, Miller." I want to call him kitten and say I'm Daddy, but even though there's no one in the corridor, I still feel exposed. "Can you let me in?"

I give it several seconds, then try knocking again. No response. He could be sleeping or in the shower. Making my mind up, I press the key card to the handle, making the little light red turn green. I hear a faint click, then push my way through.

I stand in the doorway, peering into the darkened room. "Charlie?" I whisper.

Nothing.

Enough messing around. I drop the card into the slot on the wall so I can then flick the lights on. I quickly see that I haven't woken him up because there's no one in the bed.

There's no one anywhere. No personal items, and nothing's been disturbed since housekeeping made the room up. I check the bathroom, but I already know it's going to be empty.

Charlie isn't here. I'm not sure he ever was.

And now I have *no* idea where he could be.

21

CHARLIE

THERE WAS NO WAY I WAS STAYING IN THAT ROOM WHERE Daddy's horrid brother knew where I was. I didn't want him having any more power over me than he already had.

So once the coast was clear, I turned right around and left, walking out into the night, my vision still blurry with tears.

After I manage to calm down enough to look around, I realise I have no clue where I am. But unlike the last time I was down on my luck, my phone has a decent amount of charge, and I've got almost a grand in my bank account, never mind Gilbert's check burning a hole in my pocket.

So I take some deep breaths and do an internet search for the nearest hotel. There's one within walking distance that apparently has vacancies. The nightly rate makes me gasp, but I consider the price of my dignity and decide it's not too bad after all.

It's just for one night. Tomorrow I'll decide what to do with…well. With the rest of my life, I guess. But right now, I just need to stop and pull myself together.

It all makes sense, I suppose. I fell into this thing so fast with Daddy. Naturally, it would all fall apart in the blink of an eye as well.

I paw at my throat, missing my collar far more keenly than I ever did at work. Probably because I know it's gone forever. Daddy gave it to me as a promise, and I've broken my side of the deal.

I said I was his, and then I went and left him.

To protect him, I think savagely as I scrub my face with my free hand. The other is holding my shopping bag. It feels heavy, even though it's barely half-full. Probably because everything is heavy on my heart right now.

The receptionist at the new hotel is nice. It's not too late in the evening—just gone ten thirty. Besides, this is London on a Friday night. A lot of people are only just getting going. She happily books me into a room and gives me a key card, telling me to enjoy my stay. I manage to smile at her without bursting into tears, so I'd say that's a win.

My room is so quiet and still. I perch on the end of the bed for a while, wondering what the hell I'm going to do.

Sadly, I think I'll have to cash that cheque. I hate taking Gilbert's money, but if I'm going to survive, I can't afford to throw away more money than I've ever seen attached to my name in my life. What he's given me is more than Mum's inheritance, even.

I'd rather have my mum than her money. The same way I'd rather have Daddy than his brother's pay-off. But this is my life, and I should be used to it giving me lemons by now.

I curl up on my side and stare at the walls for a while longer. It's getting to the time when Daddy would be due home from work. I manage to put my phone on airplane mode before dissolving into a fresh wave of grief, thinking of him coming through the door and realising that I'm not there. He's going to be so confused. So hurt. I didn't even have time to leave a note—not that I imagine Gilbert would have let me write one anyway.

If Daddy calls me, I know I won't be strong. I had to leave to protect him, but my resolve will crumble if I hear his voice.

I'll probably never hear his voice again.

I don't know how long I cry for, but after a while, my head starts hurting. So I calm myself enough to get up and find a box of tissues to blow my nose. Then I force myself to down a glass of tap water.

As I sit back on the bed, I spy something in my measly bag of possessions. My cat ears. I sniffle and shake as I lift them out, turning them over in my hands. Then I slip them on my head and lie back down again. I like the way the tips of the band press against my skull. My hand raises to my exposed neck again. The ears aren't as good as my collar, but they make me feel slightly more like myself. I just wish I could be a kitten again. All my problems melted away when I could leave Charlie behind for a little while.

But why can't I do that now?

I sit up with a frown as I think. I can't be Daddy's kitty anymore—and that hurts like hell—but could I still be a kitten just for me? There are clubs for that sort of thing—like Daddy was turning Bootleg into. I bite my lip and look at my phone. If I'm fast, I could risk a quick internet search.

I want to avoid Soho. It's not like Daddy owns the whole area or anything, but it just feels too painful because of my association with Bootleg. However, Daddy's mentioned a place in Vauxhall a few times that was inspiring some of his refurb. I bite my lip as I take my phone off airplane mode and search for the address as fast as possible.

I don't know if I'm disappointed or not when I don't get a call, but as I put the airplane mode back on having found the information I need, I tell myself that it's for the best. I'm not sure my heart believes that, but for now, I have to listen to my head.

Or get out of my head.

The club is called Chain and is about a half-hour journey away from here. The tube will still be running for hours, and seeing as it's a Friday, there will be an extra late service as well. Or if not, I know my way around more than one night bus timetable. But I'm feeling nervous about going to a new place all by myself.

What is my alternative? Lie here in the dark and cry myself to sleep? Or worse, spend hours not sleeping and feeling wretched for the way I've treated Daddy? I've pretty much already convinced myself he's going to hate me. I'm going to need to block his number and move on and try and leave all that pain behind.

That will take time. If I'm honest, I'm not sure if my heart will ever fully recover. But I need to escape tonight, right now. Alcohol seems like a bad idea. I'm certain it'll take about one and a half piña coladas before I drunk-dial Daddy and beg him to forgive me and take me back. I can't risk that.

But I could find some place to be a kitten for a while. I've read that spanking is an amazing way to find subspace and get a cathartic release at the same time. The idea of being hurt—especially by a stranger—scares me a lot. But I'm desperate.

Decision made, I stand and slip the ears under the waistband of my jeans and also under my T-shirt. I'm just a teeny bit happy about the idea of being a kitten again. I don't think I can manage 'excited' right now. However, I'll take anything that isn't soul-deep despair.

I'm not confident enough to wear the ears on the tube, though. But I also remember what Daddy said about public kink and consent, so it's best to keep them hidden for now.

Tears threaten to spill again as I think of all the loving

things Daddy taught me. But I shake them off and swallow the lump in my throat. It's time to be numb again and make myself operate on autopilot. I make sure I have my room card as well as my headphones so I can distract myself with really loud music for the journey, then head back out the door.

All I need to do is get to the club, and then hopefully, I can be kitten Charlie again and leave all this terrible heartache behind.

Even if it's only for a little while.

22

MILLER

I STAND OUTSIDE IN THE NIGHT AIR FOR SOME TIME, JUST staring into the middle distance and sitting with this utter sense of failure that's consumed me.

I don't care what Gil said. I still don't believe Charlie would betray me. But I'm starting to think that my brother was yet another thing in this world that I should have protected my kitten from.

Memories of that night we first met creep into my mind. Charlie was so fucking scared with nowhere to go and not a friend in the world. Well, he bloody has his *best* friend right here. I just don't know where to look. I comfort myself that thanks to me, he's not penniless, but that just opens up the possibilities of where he could go, not limit them.

Good for him. Bad for me.

I wonder if I should go back and wait for him, but I know I'll go mad. Or drink myself into a stupor. Or both.

I left his key under the front doormat, so he can let himself in if I'm not there, meaning I don't *have* to return home. But I realise Charlie doesn't actually know that, so I pull out my phone from my pocket. My heart leaps as I see a text notification, but it's just from Paul telling me he's thinking of me and that he's sure Charlie will surface soon.

In that moment, I quite appreciate a bit of Daddying for myself.

I hit Charlie's number for the dozenth time that evening, but this time I actually stop and leave an answerphone message. I was so determined to hear his voice and speak to him that I haven't done that until now. But he needs to know I'm still looking after him. That I'm desperately searching for him.

That I still love him.

"Kitten, it's Daddy," I say as soon as I hear the beep. "Sweetheart, I'm so worried. Whatever my shithead brother said to you to scare you, it doesn't matter. He's a liar who only cares about his reputation and his money. I only care about *you.* If you get this before I can find you, I left your key under the front doormat so you can let yourself in. Please come home. Please call me. I…I'm so worried for you."

I close the call and screw my eyes shut for a second. I was going to tell him that I loved him for the first time in a bloody voicemail. I'm glad I didn't. He needs to see my face when I say it. I want to see how he feels for myself.

I hope to hear him say it right back and mean it with all his heart.

I scrub my face, then make sure my phone is both off silent and the vibrate is on, so I definitely don't miss any calls or texts. What the hell do I do now?

There's only one other address that I have to connect to my baby kitten. However, I can't imagine he'd go back home to his stepfather.

But…would that arsehole maybe know something? Or could I find a clue there to somewhere else Charlie might go? I chew my lip and reason that it's a long shot, but I honestly don't have any other ideas right now, and I hate standing around.

I hunt through the information I have from setting up Charlie's new bank accounts and other things, finding his stepdad's address. Then I summon another Uber, not caring that it's peak rates on a Friday night.

My baby is worth every penny.

Luckily, my driver isn't chatty, and he has his music on low. It leaves me to stew in my thoughts. I knew my brother was a complete dick, but I didn't think he hated me this much. Maybe becoming CEO has already made the power rush to his head, and he's just trying to control every single aspect of his life around him to the nth degree. He always was a vicious bully who became genuinely outraged when the world didn't bend to his every whim.

I'm sure he sees my happiness as something he has a right to dictate.

Good lord. At least Charlie inherited his fucked-up family member. I'm related by blood to mine.

I chew my thumbnail and wonder for a brief second if he isn't actually better off running from me. The two of us might be able to talk this through, but will my brother ever stop dogging us? Trying to ruin our lives or make us disappear? I can't honestly say for sure. I just know that I'm not taking Gil's twisted word for it. If this is the end of the line for me and Charlie, I want to hear that from *his* mouth. Nobody else's.

I rub my chest as if that could dispel the pain that's been lodged there ever since I walked through my front door. I'm not a religious man, but I have to have faith that my kitten and I still have a chance.

The driver drops me off in front of a row of dilapidated terraced houses. The big blue bin on the weedy front patio is overflowing and there's another box half-full of beer cans and bottles next to it. I raise my eyebrows. At least he knows how to recycle, I suppose.

I'm oddly nervous as I knock on the door. I'm not really sure what I'm going to say or even what the hell I'm doing here. All I know is that I have to try.

For Charlie.

The man who jerks open the door is solid-looking but not all that tall. His beard is neatly trimmed, and his balding head shaved close. His shirt looks new and crisp. He slips his hands into his pockets and tilts his head as he considers me. I can't help but wonder how far my expensive suit is factoring into his opinion of me right now.

"Hello?" he greets me civilly.

"Giovanni Scarpa?" I ask.

He nods. "That's me. How can I help?"

"I'm a friend of Charlie's. I was wondering if you'd heard from him."

Ah, there we go. Giovanni's face immediately darkens. "Whatever trouble he's gotten himself into, it isn't my concern. Piss off."

He tries to shut the door on me, but I was prepared for bullshit. I thrust my foot in the way and grab the edge, forcing the door back a few inches and blocking his ability to shut me out. "I'm not finished," I growl.

"Yes, you are!" he bellows, getting all up in my face. "Unless you want me to call the police for trespassing on private property, assault, and breaking and entering!"

I smile at his bravado. Oh, yes. This is a bully who's used to getting his own way.

"Sure, call them," I say calmly. "We can have a chat about how you robbed your stepson of his entire inheritance and made him homeless."

"That money was mine—*is* mine," he snarls with perfectly white teeth. "He owed me."

I laugh gently. "Oh, Mr Scarpa. You may have thought you left Charlie with nothing, but I'm looking after him now, and I have a ridiculous amount of money and some of the best lawyers in the city on speed dial. I wonder how long it would take them to prove that you broke several laws. You'd have to give the money back at the very least, if not pay a fine as well or perhaps even serve some prison time." I shrug nonchalantly. "Who knows?"

His eyes narrow as he glares at for me a second. "What do you care? You his dad now?"

"Something like that," I say in amusement.

He looks me up and down again. "What do you *want?* I'm not paying that money back. It's mine."

"Whilst we may disagree on that front, he doesn't need his mother's money—for now. I'm asking you if he's contacted you tonight."

He scoffs. "I haven't heard from him since he moved out. Apparently, he finally listened to me. Maybe he's not so thick after all."

I step up so both feet are just inside the door, giving this arsehole my best loom. To be fair, he does shrink away a little. "He's a brilliant young man who is already thriving now he's out from under your thumb. But that's beside the point. If you haven't heard from him, then that brings me to the second reason for my visit. May I come in?"

I don't wait for an answer. I just push past him as he splutters in outrage. "No, you may not!" he yells.

"I'm going to Charlie's room and recovering the personal effects that you also stole from him," I say, not bothering to look over my shoulder as I head up the stairs. That hadn't originally been part of my plan, but I might not have long to poke about in his stuff to look for clues. So if I grab as much as I can, that has the added bonus of returning some things to my kitten that might be sentimental.

If he ever comes home.

"Get out, now!" Gio tries threatening me.

"Either you give me five minutes peace, or I call the police," I say pleasantly as I get to the landing.

It's easy to work out what room is which. There's one with a made bed, the next is a bathroom, and the last one is filled with cardboard boxes. Presumably, Giovanni was getting rid of Charlie's stuff out of spite. Good, that means I've got here in time.

Charlie's stepdad doesn't reply. He just grunts and folds his arms, watching me as I enter the room.

There are only three boxes. The walls are bare, and the bed is stripped. My heart aches for my little kitten. His life before me looks so small and empty. There is absolutely no love between these four walls.

I start rummaging through each box. One is clothes, the other is old schoolwork, and the last is all the other odds and ends, including his passport, which I give a mental fist bump for. I'll feel much better having that back in Charlie's possession than I will his stepfather's.

My heart threatens to break, though, when I see the well-loved teddy bear thrown carelessly in with everything else. There's also a gorgeous photo of my baby when he was younger with a woman who I guess to be his mother. They both look so happy. It's gut-wrenching.

"Oh, Charlie. Where *are* you?" I whisper miserably.

I take a shaky breath and brace myself. I'm not going to have the time to find anything useful here, but I can at least try and do right by my kitten.

I hope that Charlie isn't overly fond of his old essays on the British Empire, and I leave the schoolwork behind. Then I balance the other two boxes one on top of the other and heft them out of the room. He might want to throw it all away if it just reminds him of his old life, but at least this way he has a *choice.*

"Oi, you can't—" Giovanni tries to tell me. I just sidestep him and head down the stairs.

"I'll be in touch, Mr Scarpa," I say indifferently. "If I were you, I wouldn't go spending any more of Charlie's money. His mother left him that inheritance, not you. My lawyers will wring every penny back from you, even if it takes years. Thank you for your time."

I almost expect him to put his hands on me. To shout and try and grab Charlie's stuff. But he just goes quiet. When I turn around, he's stopped in the middle of the stairs. I kind of enjoy how defeated he looks.

Without another word, I take Charlie's things out into the night and walk down the road. Once I'm back on the busier, better-lit high street, I pause to put the boxes down on the ground and get my phone out. The adrenaline is already fading, and the high of my success is giving way to worry about Charlie once more. There's also some healthy resentment towards my brother as well for putting us in this mess.

I decide it's finally time to go home. I can wait for Charlie whilst I sift through his miscellaneous box and see if I can find anything useful. Bile threatens to rise in my throat as I realise despite my victory just now, I'm no closer to finding him and making sure he's safe. But what else can I do?

I've got the Uber app open, ready to hit my home address, when Paul's number pops up, and the ringtone just about makes me jump out of my skin. It shows how highly strung I am. I take a breath and rub my forehead before answering. I assume he's calling for an update, and I steel myself to deliver the disappointing news.

"Hey, Paul," I say heavily. "Still no luck, I'm afraid."

"Boss! Boss!" he cries, so animated I almost drop the phone in surprise. "I think I've got something."

"What?" I ask, trying not to raise my voice or my hopes.

"I got the word out with my guys to look for any new kittens on the scene tonight," he tells me in a rush. "I had a hunch, y'know? Well, my mate only went and spotted a boy who got to Chain about fifteen minutes ago that could very well be your Charlie. Photos are against company policy, but from the description it might be him. Right sort of build and age. Thick brown hair and a pair of nice-looking ears. I'm not promising it won't be a goose chase, but I thought you should know—"

"No, no," I'm already talking over him. "That's fantastic. Thank you, Paul. I'll head there right now!"

My heart is in my throat as I close the call and quickly pull up the new destination in the Uber app. I'm torn between hoping it's Charlie and worried sick that he's gone to Chain by himself. It's a decent enough place, but not the kind of establishment a young novice should be wandering into alone, especially not if he's in any kind of emotional state.

A car accepts my ride, but it's five minutes away.

"Fuck!" I cry out in frustration, not wanting to waste a single minute. But there's nothing I can do but wait and hope if it is Charlie, that he's still there when I arrive. And that he's not in any trouble.

Any *more* trouble.

23

CHARLIE

THE LOW LIGHTING IS HELPING QUITE A BIT TO GET ME OUT OF my own head. I wish I could have a drink or two, but I know that's a really bad idea if I'm planning on getting kinky.

But, oh, god. I'm so nervous.

I sip a pineapple juice instead, pretending it's a piña colada. I look around the main room, wondering if I should just give up and go home. This place is different to Daddy's bar. There's no stage with pole or a dance floor. There are several sofas and chairs with people sitting around talking and flirting. So much flirting. There are a number of rooms as well with a *lot* of different noises coming from them.

I look down at my rubber bracelet. It's pink, so it means I want to play. I was so tongue tied with the guy at the door who asked me what I wanted and got annoyed when I didn't know. I'm pretty certain it's not the one that means I want to have sex. That makes me feel light-headed considering sleeping with someone who isn't Daddy. I just want to be a kitten.

Is that even possible without my Daddy, though? He was the one who brought that side out of me. I wanted to be *his* kitty. Am I really into kink, or was I just kinky with Daddy?

I see other people have blue, green, and yellow bands, which all mean different things, but I'm not sure what. I'm in over my head. And yet putting on my ears and having people look my way is giving me a small boost, even if it's just fleeting.

This was the point of coming out here tonight. To see if I can start to work out what my life's going to look like in a world without Daddy. Without my stepdad breathing down my neck as well, but I was already experiencing that with Daddy, and it was wonderful.

Now I'm alone, and it's scary and hollow and it's taking everything I've got to hold myself together right now.

Tomorrow will be easier. And the day after that. I just have to get through each moment until my heart stops feeling like it's going to drag me down to the depths of the ocean where I can't breathe or see or feel.

Fuck. I scrub at my eyes, willing myself not to cry again. Nobody's going to be interested in me if I'm a weepy mess. I could have put these ears on alone at the hotel and saved myself the faff of getting on the tube. No. I want to see if I can play *with* someone. Someone who might help me slip properly into sub space so I can forget about Charlie and all his problems and just be a kitten for a while.

I've been sitting for a bit, and my drink is pretty much done. So I muster up my courage to get to my feet—who knew standing would be such an act of bravery? But it is—and take my empty glass back to the bar. Then I try not to overthink and just keep walking to take a look inside the room for impact play.

There are a few pieces of equipment that honestly look like medieval torture devices to me. But there are people in various states of undress tied to them getting spanked and flogged and smacked with paddles, and even the ones who are crying seem to be having an amazing time. My skin tingles just looking at them.

I think it's okay to watch because a lot of people are, most of them sitting around on yet more sofas and armchairs. Some people are touching themselves or others suggestively, but they don't have anything too naughty out. That's for different rooms…I think. I hate how clueless I am.

I almost fall down the rabbit hole of wishing Daddy was here. He was supposed to guide me through this new world, after all. But he can't be here. It's not fair or safe for me to be near him.

Actually—the fact that I *like* all this dirty stuff is *why* I have to stay away from him. Maybe if I didn't want to be a kitten and have my bum smacked like a pervert, we could be together.

But…no. I can't magically make myself older, and Gilbert said that's part of the problem as well.

"Like what you see?"

The voice in my ear makes me jump and grab my chest. The man it belonged to chuckles and sidles closer to me. He's in jeans and a button-down, kind of like Daddy's style, and I'm ashamed how much I want to hug him just because of that. He's not Daddy, though, so I remember my manners and smile at him. He's blond—also different to Daddy.

Wow, I'm going to *have* to stop comparing every man I look at to Daddy. It's not fair on them, and it's only going to torture me.

Miller. Not Daddy. There we go. It hurts, but from now on, that's what I have to call him.

"Um, hi," I squeak.

The man smiles down at me. "Aren't you adorable? What's your name, kitten?"

I'm not sure I like hearing anyone who isn't Da-*Miller* call me that. But I guess I'll just have to get used to it.

"Charlie," I say, just about managing to make it not sound like a question.

"Spencer," the man says with a nod. "Do you want to come sit with me? I'd like to get to know you."

My heart is like a bloody jackhammer in my chest. I'm so nervous, and I try reminding myself that this was what I wanted. This is the *reason* I came here. Yet there's a part of me that wants to run.

"O-okay," I make myself say, even forcing a little smile. I have to give someone else a try, so I follow him over to a sofa that was just vacated and sit beside him. He drapes his arm over the back, but it's not actually touching me, so I try and relax. He's just being friendly.

"These are cute," he says with a flick to my ears. I flinch but try and cover it up with a laugh.

"Um, thanks. They're new." *I'm new.*

"Is that so?" Spencer asks. "And what kind of kitty are you?" he also asks before I get a chance to reply.

"A good one," I say, disregarding that I loved being naughty for Daddy. Miller—*urgh!* I think naughty is something I'll have to work up to again. Right now, I just want to be good and be *told* I'm good. After doing such a horrible thing and feeling so sad, I'm really craving some praise.

But Spencer hums and moves closer, pressing our thighs together and dropping his arm onto my shoulders.

My heart skips a beat and not in a good way. That urge to run is fighting me again, but I make myself stay put. This is Domineering, right? He's supposed to take charge and boss me around. I need to stop being such a scaredy-cat.

"I think you're a *bad* kitty," Spencer says. "You need a

master to wrap a collar tightly around your throat and spank you until you know who's in charge."

Oh, god. I know that's supposed to be sexy, but I'm really starting to panic now. I can't be a prick tease, though, can I? So I let out a nervous giggle and try not to flinch as he starts stroking up and down my arm.

"I'm sorry," I whisper.

"I bet you are," Spencer scoffs. "A sweet little thing like you parading around getting everyone's attention. What a slut."

The lump rises in my throat again, and the tears that have been so close to the surface since Gilbert walked into my life teeter on the brim of my lower lids.

"I'm sorry," I whimper again. "I'll be good."

"Oh, I'll make you be good, kitten," Spencer growls, turning his body so it's more inclined to mine. I'm feeling pretty trapped. "In fact, I think I'll make you suck my cock. You're a little slut, after all. You'll love that, won't you?"

I gasp and can't stop the tears from falling, much to my horror. "No," I gasp.

But Spencer just laughs. "Yes, you will because I say you will. See? I knew you were a bad kitten. But it's okay. Master is here to take you in hand."

His mouth is getting dangerously close to mine, and I don't know what to do. We didn't talk about safe words, but I'm not honestly sure if this is my fault. I agreed to sit with him. I'm wearing the pink band. It would be mean and rude to scuttle away from him like I want to. But he's kind of got me caged now with his other hand holding my shoulder. I'm pinned down against the couch. Maybe it's best if I just do what he says.

Maybe that's safest.

"I'm sorry," I say with a sniffle. "I promise I didn't mean to be bad. I'll be good."

Spencer bashes his nose against mine, and I wince. "I don't want you to be good, though, kitten. Master wants you to be a bad little slut. Now, come with me, and I can get on with fucking your throat."

I grimace and squeeze my eyes shut. *"No,"* I say, surprising myself. I want to be good. I want to forget about Daddy. But I really, *really* don't want to do that. "I'm sorry, but no. Um...*red.*"

Spencer leans back a little, but his body against mine is stiff. I peek up and see him scowling. "What the fuck?" he utters. "You're safe wording over *that?* I didn't do anything. Why the fuck are you even here if you don't want to play?"

I try and hold back the sob, rubbing my chest and dropping my gaze to the floor. "I don't know. It was a mistake. I'm so sorry. I didn't mean to lead you on."

"Well, you did," Spencer replies grumpily. "Fine. Fuck it. We don't have to play, but you at least owe me a blow job." I start shaking my head, bile rising up my gullet as he crowds over me again. "Yes, you do," he insists. "Come on. Stop making this weird. Let's just go into the other room, kitten."

"No," I say a little louder. "Red! I don't—"

Suddenly, Spencer is gone.

In fact, he's sprawled on his arse on the floor, blinking up in shock.

But he's not looking at me.

"The boy said *no,*" Daddy snarls.

24

MILLER

IT'S FUNNY CHARLIE SHOULD MENTION RED, BECAUSE THAT'S all I'm seeing.

"What the fuck?" the sleazy guy says incredulously up at me. "What the hell is your problem?"

Everyone in the room is watching, and security have come over. But I feel oddly calm as I stare the creep down. "He said no *and* safe worded. What's *your* problem?"

The guy splutters. "We were playing! I didn't—"

"All right, mate," the large bouncer says. He leans down to hook his hand under the sleazeball's armpit and hauls him up. "Let's go."

"No, but I didn't—" the guy continues to protest, but the bouncer is immune as he escorts him towards the door.

People begin to talk again, and my mist of pure rage starts to ebb away.

I take a breath, then finally turn back around to see my baby kitten trembling on the sofa.

"Daddy," he says, bursting into tears. *"I'm so sorry."*

I'm over to him in a flash, wrapping him in my arms as he sobs. "It's okay," I tell him, the relief finally flowing through me like a dam rupturing. He's here. He's safe. Everything's going to be all right. "Daddy's got you. You're okay."

He shakes his head vehemently. "It's not okay!" he cries.

Luckily, the music is loud enough to swallow his words, so the people around us shouldn't hear much. I'd prefer this reunion to be in private, but it also has to happen *now*, and I'm not moving.

"Yes, it is, kitten," I say firmly. "Would Daddy ever lie to you?"

"No," he says uncertainly, followed by a gulp. "But…your brother said I was going to ruin you. He said I had to leave. Otherwise, you'd lose all your money, and your family business would go under because…" He breaks out into a fresh wave of sobs. "Because I'm too young, and I like being your kitten too much and if the papers find out—"

"Whoa, whoa, whoa," I say, hugging him tighter against me to try and calm him down. I fucking *knew* Gil had played some kind of mind game like that. I'm going to deal with him in the very near future, but all I care about right now is Charlie. "I'm sorry. My brother is an arsehole. He threatened me, too."

"Really?" Charlie says, blinking spikey lashes as he looks up at me.

I nod. "Actually, he threatened *you*. He's convinced I need to break up with you and sell Bootleg to protect the family and business reputations."

"Exactly," Charlie says miserably. "That's why I left. To protect you. I'd *never* hurt you, Daddy! So you need to let me leave!"

He pushes at my chest, but I grab his wrists, and he immediately stills, looking back into my eyes. "I don't give a fuck what my brother says," I say calmly and firmly, not letting Charlie avert his gaze. "When I got home and you were gone, it was the worst moment of my life. I'll do *anything* to keep you by my side, baby kitty."

He just stares at me for a second. "I'm so sorry," he whispers, his lip trembling. "I knew you'd hate me when you realised—"

I can't help but laugh and cup my hands around his face. "I could *never* hate you, kitten. I was *terrified.* I didn't know where you were or if you were afraid or hurt. All that matters is that I've found you now." *Just in time,* I add to myself, a fresh wave of anger crashing over me as I recall that fucker's hands on my boy.

"How *did* you find me?" Charlie asks with a sniff.

I brush tears away from his cheeks with my thumbs. "Paul asked his friends to look out for you, and one of them spotted you coming in here."

Charlie lets out a sigh and nods. "I'm glad you found me," he says in a small voice. "I was trying to protect you, but I was so sad. I wanted to be a kitten again. But that man was horrible."

His face crumples and I pull him to me in a hug again. "He's gone now. I promise."

Charlie nods his head against my chest, and I just hold him for a while. "I've got an Uber waiting outside," I say after a bit. "How about we get out of here and I can take you home?"

He shivers against me. "You really want me to come back to your house after what I did to you?"

I'm already shaking my head before he finishes speaking. "You didn't do *anything* to me. It was all Gilbert. Of course I want you back in *our home* because that's where you belong." I swallow and make myself pause for a second. "Only if that's what you want, though?"

He grabs my shirt in a startling panic. "I want that more

than anything, Daddy!" he cries. "But only if you're sure it's safe. If I ruined you—"

"I won't let that happen," I say, meaning it with all my soul. "Gil can say what he likes. He's got the power to invent terrible things, I know. But the truth is you and I aren't doing *anything* wrong. We're two consenting adults who…" Oh, fuck it. If tonight's taught me anything, it's that I can't take anything for granted. "Two adults who *love* each other. And that's the most beautiful thing in the world."

His mouth pops open, and for a second, it looks like he's forgotten how to breathe. I kind of know the feeling. But then he exhales in a big whoosh and touches his hand to his chest. "You love me?"

"So much," I say with all the sincerity I possess. "I don't know what's going to happen with my family, Charlie kitten. All I do know is that I want you there by my side, every day. You're the light of my life and I honestly don't know what I'd do without you. So long as that's what you want, too."

He laughs. It's wet and sweet. He also hiccups, and my heart wants to burst out of my chest with happiness. "I love you so much, Daddy," he says. It's like the clouds parting for the sunshine on a rainy day. "I want to be with you. To be your kitten and your boyfriend and…I don't even know. I just want to be near you."

I cuddle him close to me, kissing his hair and fighting the lump that fills my throat. "I just want you near, too, sweetheart. We'll find a way. If we're together, everything else will be okay."

I can't promise disaster won't befoul us or that my brother won't be malicious. But all the fears I felt in the club pale in comparison to thinking I might never see Charlie again or that he doesn't want me anymore. Of course I'd respect his wishes if he really wanted to break up, but I'll fight like hell if there is even a chance of us being able to work things out.

If he wants to be with me like he's saying, I'll take on the devil himself to make that happen.

Or my brother, but he is basically Satan to me at this point.

"Come on," I say to my poor kitten. He's been through enough tonight. "Let's go home."

"My stuff is at my hotel," Charlie says as I help him to stand.

"So you checked into a different one?" I ask. He blinks at me, and I chuckle as we begin walking towards the exit. "I know my brother's regular haunt. I was so excited when I got there and he had a reservation, but you were already gone."

Charlie bites his lip and stares at me. "You really looked that hard for me?"

I scoff. "Of course. I couldn't get through on your phone, so I started a manhunt."

"I put it on airplane mode," he confesses. "Gilbert said he was monitoring you and that if we spoke on the phone, he'd know." He shakes his head. "I wanted to call you so badly, and I knew I'd pick up if I saw your number, so airplane mode seemed like the best option."

I sigh, hating my brother even more. He really scared the shit out of my baby. "It's okay. I totally understand. I love how brave you were, kitten. But Daddy's going to take care of you and everything now. You don't have to be alone ever again."

He hugs against my side as we walk out of the club. He pauses to give the pink bangle back with a slight grimace on his face. I *hate* that he almost had a terrible experience. But I remind myself that I got there in time and everything's all right.

My Uber driver was prepared to wait, and luckily found a

rare parking spot around the corner from the club. He's watching a video on his phone of pandas rolling down slides and hills when I tap on the glass to let him know I've returned. Then Charlie and I slide into the back seats.

Charlie gasps when he sees the boxes. "What the…?"

"Gil's hotel wasn't the only place I tried looking for you," I admit as I first help him with his seat belt then fasten my own. Charlie's in the middle, pressed against me, with the two boxes on the other side of him.

We give the Uber driver the address for the hotel, then my house. As he pulls away from the kerb, Charlie reaches into the top box, going straight for the photo of him and his mum.

"You went to see my stepdad?" he asks, shaking his head.

I can't help but smirk. "Yes, I did. And when I realised he hadn't heard from you, I took it upon myself to rescue the things he'd boxed up to throw away."

"Teddy!" Charlie cries out in delight, swapping the picture frame for his stuffed bear. He hugs it tightly and snuggles up against my side. "You're too good to be true, Daddy," he says softly so our driver won't hear over his dance music.

I sigh and kiss my baby's head. "I assure you, kitten. I'm true and real, and not going anywhere. You're mine, and I need it to stay the way."

"Yes, Daddy," Charlie says sleepily but with contentment. "All yours."

Good. That's all I need to know.

We can deal with whatever else comes our way later. For now, we're back together, and that's all that matters.

25

CHARLIE

It's kind of surreal as we walk through the door of Daddy's house. I thought I'd never see it again. Daddy is carrying my boxes, and I've got the shopping bag with the few possessions I took when I was forced to leave here. I place it down as he kicks the door shut, then he puts the boxes by the bag so his hands are free to properly lock the door.

Shutting the rest of the world out. It's just us two, and my heart soars.

A couple of hours ago, everything was so dark. But Daddy found me like some kind of white knight and brought back the light. I'm still scared of what might happen, but he says it's okay, and he wants me to stay, and I have to admit I'm not strong enough to disagree. I just hope I don't ruin him like Gilbert said I would.

Daddy made it very clear that's what his family does. His dad and now his brother will lie their way through anything to get what they want. Daddy explained that Gilbert is just a bigot who wants to keep the family reputation all white-picket fence with traditional wives and children and squeaky-clean portfolios.

But Daddy's right. We're not doing anything *wrong* here. Gilbert just doesn't like it. There's a difference.

And it's time to put things right.

I wrap my fingers around my collar in the bowl where I left it, gingerly lifting it up. I wonder if it's still mine, and look to Daddy.

Wordlessly, he offers his hands out to take it. Our fingers brush as I pass it over, then I sink to my knees, looking up at the man I love with reverence.

He *loves* me. How bad can life get when that's true?

Gently, he slips the collar around my neck, kneeling before me so he can fasten the buckle. A deep sense of rightness and belonging settles over me as I feel its weight. But then Daddy leans forwards and kisses me softly. Our first kiss since I left and thought I'd never see him again, let alone ever feel his perfect mouth claiming mine once more. I whimper and cling to his shoulders.

"It's okay, kitten," he mumbles against my lips. "I've got you. You're safe. We're home."

"Daddy," I say as if making myself believe that he's really here.

Our tender moment is interrupted by a solid headbutt to my arm that makes me laugh.

"Hello, Florence," I say fondly as she screams at me. "I know. I'm so sorry. I should never have left."

She purrs as she rubs herself against me and Daddy, clearly telling us both off but also letting us know that she's happy we sorted things out.

Me, too, girl.

Daddy helps me off the floor, kissing my cheek sweetly as I steady myself on my feet. Then he picks up the boxes again, and I take my bag. We head up the stairs, also accompanied by Florence, who does her best to trip us up.

It's good to be home.

We drop off my things in the living room, then Daddy takes me into the kitchen and insists I have a big glass of water. I didn't quite realise how thirsty I was until I've downed the whole thing. I take a couple of breaths and notice my hands are slightly shaking, so I put the empty glass down. Daddy slips his bigger hands around mine, caressing my skin with his thumbs.

"How are you feeling, kitten?"

I sigh and look up at him. That name felt so wrong from Gilbert and Spencer, but that's all I want to be for Daddy. His special little kitten.

"Good," I say honestly. "Tired."

"It's late," Daddy says with a laugh. "We've had quite the night. I say it's time for bed."

I nod. He won't get any protest from me.

He pauses a moment to find my toothbrush and phone charger in my bag, then he takes me by the hand and leads me towards the landing. "Night, Florence," I say to the cat, who is practically falling asleep on the spot. I wonder if she's been restless this whole time we've been gone. Guilt creeps inside me, but I try and soothe it with a promise that I'll never do that to her again.

Daddy and I head upstairs to his—*our*—bedroom, where he herds me like a sheepdog into the bathroom and even puts toothpaste on my brush for me, watching as I give my mouth a scrub. Once I've rinsed, he gently escorts me back into the bedroom and has me stand in front of him whilst he sits on the edge of the bed. Then he slides his fingers under my jumper and pulls it over my head.

It's then that I realise I've still got my ears on, and giggle.

Daddy smiles up at me once the jumper is over my head, and he drops it to the floor. "What, sweet kitty?"

"I forgot I was still wearing these," I say as I bat one of the ears. "The Uber driver must have thought I was weird."

Daddy glides his hands over my hips, his fingers skimming my bare skin. "I'm sure he's seen *much* worse than an adorable, sleepy, very loved kitten in his back seat."

I giggle and hum as Daddy kisses my tummy. I card my fingers through his hair, scratching lightly against his scalp, already feeling like I've got my claws back.

I might not have my full gear on, but between my collar and ears, I'm definitely able to start falling into that blissful headspace where nothing matters but my Daddy. He'll keep me safe and love me. He knows what to do.

"What's your colour, kitten?" he asks me.

"Green, Daddy," I tell him happily.

He kisses me just under my rib cage. "What do you want tonight, baby?"

"You, Daddy." My voice catches slightly. Oh, *god.* I almost lost him.

"You have me, sweet boy," he promises. "I'll hold you all night. But do you want to just cuddle and sleep, or do you want to make love? What will soothe you right now?"

I groan and stumble against him. His arms immediately wrap around me, hugging me tightly. "Make love," I say. It sounds like I'm begging. I am, in a way. "And…Daddy?"

"Yes, kitten?" He leans back and raises his eyebrows at me.

I'm a little nervous, but after everything we've been through tonight, I reason with myself what's the worst that can happen? I trust my Daddy. I can ask him anything.

"Would you…do you know how to…um…?"

"What, sweetheart?" he prompts me gently.

"I think I'd like to be spanked," I say in a rush.

Daddy nods like he's not surprised and strokes my ticklish sides. "I know how to do that right, yes," he says warmly. "Can I ask why you'd like that? What kind of spanking is it?"

I chew my lip, thinking back to the room in the club earlier and recalling what I've read online. "I want to cry," I say softly, looking down at the carpet. "I want…release."

"So it's not a punishment?" Daddy says.

I frown and look back at him. "No?" I say, but I'm unsure.

However, he shakes his head. "That's good, kitten. I was worried you thought you needed punishing, but you absolutely don't. A cathartic spanking sounds wonderful, though. Healthy, actually. Shall we get you comfy and give it a try?"

The sob sneaks up from my chest. I throw my arms around his neck and hug him tightly. "You're the best Daddy in the whole world," I mumble against his neck. "I knew you'd understand."

He rubs my back. "Of course, baby. That's my job. Taking care of you means everything to me."

I think of that arsehole back at the club who wouldn't even listen to my safe word, and wonder if I even need a spanking to cry. Daddy is the complete opposite of that. But there's something deep within me that's craving the pain. I don't know if I'll like it until I try it, but right now, I'm desperate.

Daddy finishes undressing me so I'm naked aside from my collar and ears. He takes his own clothes off, then we move so he's sat with his back against the pillows. I'm lying face down over his lap, my cock nestled comfortably between his legs. He makes sure I have a pillow for my head and that I'm comfy, then strokes his palm against the curve of my bum.

"Are you ready, kitten?" he asks.

I nod and close my eyes. "Yes, Daddy. I'm ready."

I hear his hand whoosh through the air, then gasp at the sting of it hitting my cheek. Tingles fly all over my body, and I groan.

"How was that?" Daddy checks with me.

"Lovely," I say with a sigh.

It's such a strange feeling. How can I be on edge but calm at the same time? I'm not sure, but as Daddy drops his hand again and again on my bum and thighs, the feeling increases. I gasp and yelp and meow, letting everything out. It's not long before I'm crying.

And I mean crying.

It's like the floodgates open and all my complicated emotions from the evening come pouring out. Tears stream down my face, and my nose runs, making the pillow wet under my head. But I don't care. With each blow, it's like I become freer, less burdened. All the badness is slipping away.

"Kitten?" Daddy says.

I blink, pulling myself out from my stupor. He's produced a bottle from somewhere and is squeezing a creamy liquid onto the palm he was using to spank me. "Hmm?" I say. It's about all I'm capable of right now.

He chuckles softly. "It's over. You did so well. How do you feel?"

I moan loudly as he begins rubbing the cooling lotion over my sore bum. "So good," I say truthfully. It's like I've orgasmed, even though I haven't. A new kind of release that I've never felt before. "I loved it."

"Good," Daddy says, sounding proud of me. "That's so good, baby boy."

He leans over and gets a tissue from the box to hand to me, and I manage to wipe my face and blow my nose. I feel clean. Expunged.

The lotion is all over my thighs as well, so when Daddy shifts us onto our sides and spoons me, his hard cock slides gorgeously between my legs. His thrusts are gentle against my hot cheeks, but I feel his desire all the same as he kisses my neck and reaches over to start stroking my hardening cock. I feel like after everything this evening, it's not going to take me long to orgasm.

"My beautiful baby," Daddy murmurs into my ear. "So good for coming back to Daddy. So perfect and sweet. Daddy loves you so much, kitten. You're safe here. I've got you."

I make a keening noise as I jut my hips, loving how his cock feels against my skin and how his hand is amazing as he strokes me harder. I turn my head, searching for his mouth, which he gives me for a messy, open-mouthed kiss.

"Daddy," I whisper, just because I can.

"Kitten," he says back between kisses. "Come for me. Come for your Daddy. He loves you so much."

I cry out and close my eyes, allowing myself to surrender to his touch. I can feel my climax rushing towards me. It's so easy to embrace it here, secure in my Daddy's arms.

I shudder as I start spilling over the bedsheets, feeling Daddy's cock throbbing between my legs as he does the same. He gasps and plants kisses on my neck and shoulder, telling me he loves me and how good I am. I cling to him as I ride out my high. After the spanking as well as the orgasm, I'm utterly shattered and wrung out, barely able to keep my eyes open once I'm done.

"Good kitten," Daddy murmurs as he cuddles me. "Oh, fuck. I'm so happy you came back, Charlie. My kitten. You're mine, and nothing's going to change that. My beautiful boy."

"Daddy," I mumble sleepily as I try and nuzzle even closer to him.

"It's okay," he says as I succumb to my exhaustion. "Daddy's got you. Daddy will take care of everything."

I don't know much to be true and certain in my life, but I do trust that.

I've got my Daddy, so it's all going to be all right.

26

CHARLIE – TWO MONTHS LATER

"Hi, welcome to Bootleg," I say to the new patrons who have just arrived. "Table for three?"

The guys smile and nod at me as I lead them through the club. From their body language, I guess they're a throuple, and it makes me feel all warm and fuzzy inside. I love that these are the kinds of people I'm surrounded by now on a daily basis.

I quit my old job at the horrible shop pretty much immediately after all that business with Gilbert. Daddy made it very clear that he wanted me to officially move in and let him take care of me. But I soon wanted purpose, so when the opportunity came up to be a host at Bootleg, I jumped at it. Daddy and I were cautious about mixing work and home life so early on in our relationship, but so far, it's working out perfectly.

The best part—other than being able to see Daddy all the time—is that I get to be a kitten in public, and it's like I've become a whole new me. I would have never thought I was any kind of exhibitionist before, but now whenever I'm hosting, I get to strut around in all my kitten gear. I have different house and work outfits. Both always include my collar and ears, but for home I have comfier options. I like to be sexy at the club, though. Like tonight I'm wearing a beautiful black corset, tiny shorts with a luxurious tail, and thigh-high boots that have a three-inch heel, making me feel like I could stomp all over the world.

People notice me now. They never did in my old life. I love it.

In fact...tonight is very special. I'm going to be having a whole lot of people watching me intently. I'm slightly nervous but also very excited.

And it's all because of Daddy. I'm sure I never would have found this confidence by myself. I'm so grateful. The bone-deep contentment I feel when I'm kitten Charlie still makes me marvel.

I suppose I'm kind of kitten Charlie all the time in some way or another, especially once Daddy gave me a day collar that I can wear out in non-kinky public spaces. But it's different when we actually play or here at Bootleg. It's like I have an alter ego, but that confidence does bleed through into my regular life.

Like how I felt able to challenge Giovanni and get my mum's inheritance money back—with Daddy's help, of course. I didn't actually *need* the money. Daddy has more than enough. But he helped me to see it was the principle of the thing. How dare that man try to take the last gift my mum ever gave me.

In the end, the mere threat of legal action was enough to get him to cough it up. Hopefully, I'll never have to hear from him again so long as I live. That's part of old Charlie's life. There's no room for that kind of toxicity in new kitten Charlie's life.

Daddy had to wrestle with his own family issues as well, but that didn't turn out nearly as scary as we both feared they would either. He decided to fight fire with fire and privately went to see his brother's wife. As it transpired, she was fully aware of Gilbert's affairs, but the way he tried to threaten and blackmail me and Daddy was the last straw for her. Being a kick-arse lawyer, she's got the divorce already well in hand, and has helped protect us with a restraining order. She also promised to assist us with a defamation counter case in the event of Gilbert ever trying to make good on his threats to ruin us or drum up false charges, but he seems to have decided against the whole idea now.

Partly because Daddy subtly but firmly let it be known via social media that I'm his boyfriend and that he now runs Bootleg. A couple of the tabloids ran with it as a gossip piece for a few days, but ultimately, it wasn't that much of a big deal. Daddy took Gilbert's power away from him.

Gilbert also backed off because his wife and Daddy made it clear they'd make a huge noise about the family's silk company and their violation of international human rights laws if he didn't. In fact, Gilbert's even promised to start moving towards more ethical work practices, but we'll see if he makes good on that. If he values his company's reputation that much, though, I really hope he would.

Whilst all that drama was slowly dying down, Bootleg officially reopened and has been flourishing ever since. I'm so proud of Daddy and Paul for all their hard work. Since I started working here, I also now have so many friends through the club who are into the same kinds of kinky things I am. I've never had a community of my own before, but now I do.

It's wonderful.

It's crazy to think that the bar I was so terrified to creep into a couple of months ago has now become my sanctuary. I never would have predicted that this would be how my life unfolded after turning twenty-one, but I'm so glad it has.

A hand slips over my waist, and I turn with a smile to greet Daddy. "Hi," I say softly.

He beams at me like I'm a delightful surprise and not a regular employee. "Hello, kitten," he says, nuzzling our noses together. "It's time. Are you ready?"

My breath hitches, but I nod. "Yes, Daddy. I'm excited."

That's true. I'm also nervous, but Daddy assures me that's only natural. I've never done anything like this before, after all. But I want to try, and as always, I trust my Daddy.

He kisses me. I taste cherry cola on his lips. I wonder if he tastes the pineapple on mine.

He takes me by the hand and we head to one of the newly refurbished playrooms. In my heels, I'm almost as tall as he is, but he still manages to make me feel small and precious.

There's a small crowd in the room but no one else on any of the equipment. Paul put a sign on the door earlier saying there was going to be a display tonight, so people knew to wait until after to start their own play. This is the first kinky event Bootleg is running. The bar is alcohol-free tonight, and several different displays and games are going on all evening. I'm one of the first so I didn't have time to get too anxious.

As Daddy leads me to the middle of the room, however, I'm not afraid. In fact, I'm already starting to float with so many people watching me and expecting a show. I wonder if this is how actors feel on stage. I'm not really me anymore. I'm Charlie kitten.

It's funny, though. Everybody's gazes are what's making me extra confident, but as I look at Daddy, it's like there's no one else in the world but us two.

We stand in the centre of the room, and he kisses me, but this time with passion and fervour, claiming me for all to witness. He slides his fingers through my hair and squeezes my bum. "Who loves you?" he asks, his voice low and husky. So sexy.

"Daddy," I say without hesitation.

"Who's going to take care of you?"

"Daddy."

"Who's in charge?"

"Daddy."

He nods. "That's right, and no one else. No matter what you might feel or hear, Daddy's in charge of it all. Do you still want to play?"

"Yes, Daddy," I say with a big, dopey smile. I already feel drunk off him. I really am the luckiest kitty in the world.

We talked through the scene in detail earlier, so I don't need anything more as he leads me over to a small prayer bench. We stand by it, and I look down as he slides his fingers under the waistband of my shorts, pulling them over my hips. I'm not wearing anything underneath, so my half-hard cock springs free, but I'm not shy. It's exhilarating.

Carefully, we both work on sliding the shorts over my long boots. Then Daddy helps me kneel with my feet under the small, padded bench and my bare bottom sat on the cushion. He wraps a cloth blindfold over my eyes, and I feel the instant calm that comes with it. I focus on my breathing and Daddy's touch as he binds my wrists with soft cuffs.

There are murmurs all around me, but it's only Daddy's voice I tune into as he nuzzles his nose against my cheek. "What's your colour, kitten?"

"Green, Daddy," I say happily.

"Good kitty," he says proudly, and I glow. "Now, would you like some cream?"

I grin in the darkness. "Yes, Daddy," I say, my voice more eager.

He leaves me for a few moments, and then the next thing I feel is the cool touch of a ceramic bowl against my lips. Rich dairy cream flows into my mouth, but some of it spills down my chin and onto my bare chest above my PVC corset.

My boots are wipe clean as well, and there's a mat under my knees to protect the floor, so I'm not worried about making a mess.

In fact, I'm quite looking forward to it.

I gulp down more cream, but just as much spills over me. Then the bowl leaves my lips, and I wait in anticipation. Even though I'm waiting for it, I still gasp when Daddy's mouth finds my neck, and he starts kissing and licking the cream from my skin. His hand encircles my cock as well, coated in something slippery and sweet-smelling, and his palm glides over my length, getting me harder.

I pant, dropping my head back so my neck and collar are more exposed, and let out a meow. I was apprehensive about making those kinds of sounds with just Daddy a couple of months ago, but now here I am doing it in front of a room full of people. I definitely hear at least one person groan, though, so that boosts my confidence.

I am kitten Charlie, and I am in a safe space full of love.

Daddy kisses my lips again, slowing his hand down and squeezing my cock tightly. I moan into his mouth and squirm, loving feeling restricted by how I'm sitting on the bench and with my hands bound behind my back. I can't go anywhere, so I have to trust Daddy to take care of me.

And that I do.

"Are you enjoying that, pretty kitty?" Daddy asks me.

I nod. "I love it, Daddy."

He hums and licks another drop of cream from my chin. "Are you ready to be petted like a good, sweet kitty?"

I nod again, although this time I'm slightly nervous. This is the bit I'm unsure of, but facing the unknown is also giving me a thrill. I can do it. I can be a good kitty and make my Daddy proud.

"Yes, please," I rasp.

The first touch from a different hand makes me jump

slightly, but Daddy kisses my cheek. "Good boy. Pretty boy," he tells me.

I breathe in and out as more hands gently start to stroke me. Then there are a few licks and kisses all over my exposed skin, not just where there's still cream. Someone takes my hand and starts to play with my fingers.

I shiver and sob, overwhelmed by the love I feel. It's not just the caresses and kisses. It's in the air surrounding me and filling my lungs. It's seeping deep into my heart.

Daddy keeps telling me that I'm a good and pretty kitten as his hand starts moving over my hard length again, but he's not the only one who's speaking. Lots of voices whisper and murmur the same sort of things as they fuss me. I purr and meow and nuzzle my head against the touches against my face.

I'm trembling and tearful as well but in a good way. My release is building slowly, but it feels powerful. Like it's coming from deep within. I cry out as I get closer, and Daddy captures my mouth like he's savouring every little sound I make.

"Come now, kitten," he urges me. "You've been so good for Daddy and his friends. We love you. You're beautiful. Show Daddy how happy you are and give him your cream."

I gnash my teeth and thrash against the many hands stroking all over me as my climax rushes over me. I wail as my cock throbs, and I start to spill my load all over Daddy's fingers and the mat beyond. He slows his hand and kisses my mouth as I slowly come down.

"Good boy. So good."

Gradually, the other touches start to slow and stop. I feel Daddy's fingers against the blindfold around my head. He slowly lifts it, and I blink, my vision blurred to begin with in the low light of the playroom. But then I see all the people around me kneeling, crouched and standing. They're all smiling fondly, and I manage a weak laugh.

"Wow," I croak, still feeling out of it from my orgasm and the high of the whole experience.

The people start to drift away, but I don't really notice as Daddy moves to kneel in front of me, cupping either side of my face. "How was that?" he asks.

I grin, definitely punch drunk. "Amazing," I say.

"You're amazing," he tells me fondly.

I shake my head. "No, *you're* amazing," I say with another little laugh. "Thank you, Daddy. I love you."

"I love you, too," he says, then gives me a sweet kiss.

And there's no better feeling in the world than that.

EPILOGUE

MILLER – TEN MONTHS LATER

I watch Charlie splashing in the waves, his skin glistening in the brilliant sunshine.

He's so perfect it almost breaks my heart.

He waves to me on my sun lounger, and I wave back with a laugh. He'd never really been to the beach before this holiday. Now he's surrounded by tropical waters, golden sands, and palm trees for the next two weeks.

A vast improvement on his last birthday, if I do say so myself.

He shakes his thick hair and then starts pushing his way out of the water, heading back to me. I've got a fresh piña colada served in half a coconut waiting for him. His eyes light up when he sees it, but then he gets a devilish look on his face before shaking salty water droplets all over me.

"Gah!" I cry in surprise, throwing my arms up and laughing. I don't really care, though. In fact, I grab him and haul him into my lap, loving the way his body feels so cool from the sea against my hot skin. I'm under an umbrella, but there's no escaping the heat in the Caribbean. "Bad kitty."

He grins and leans down to kiss me, slow like treacle. It's

crazy to think he's the same young man as the terrified boy who walked into my life a year ago today, lashing out and teetering over the edge.

My kitten really is remarkable.

"How's being twenty-two so far?" I ask.

He plucks the wedge of pineapple off the side of his drink, licking the cocktail from it before nibbling the tip seductively. Fuck. The things I'm going to do to him when I've got him behind a closed door.

"Taylor Swift was right," he says playfully. "It's awesome."

I think that's a reference to a song title. Sometimes the age gap between us is more obvious than others, but I don't care. I love that we're always teaching each other something new. I laugh and kiss along his jaw, giving him time to eat his fruit, then rinse his hand with some water from a bottle.

I decide it's time.

"Pass me that other coconut, would you, baby?" I nod towards the one next to his drink. This coconut is still cut in half, but the top is perched on the bottom, so it still looks whole. He frowns and reaches for it, holding it out for me to take.

"Is that your drink?"

"Actually, it's for you," I say mysteriously. "Why don't you open it?"

"Another birthday present?" he accuses. "But you've already taken me on holiday. You promised you wouldn't go too crazy spoiling me."

Even after all this time together, he still worries sometimes that he's being greedy. I don't care, though. I'll always remind him that to me, taking care of him is the ultimate pleasure.

"I promised no such thing," I protest. "Now, come on. Be a good kitty for Daddy and open it."

The beach is private and currently sparsely populated, so

I don't need to worry about keeping my voice down. In fact, it's thrilling to use our pet names out in the open for a change.

Charlie narrows his eyes at me, but he does as he's told. First, he just tries to pull the coconut apart, but then he realises there's a little mechanism, so he twists it instead, and the husk pops apart.

The flesh has gone so it's just the dried shell that holds my gifts inside. There's a small box and a larger drawstring bag. "Why don't you start with that one," I say, indicating the latter.

He thoughtfully places the top of the coconut down then balances the bottom so he can lift the bag out. He opens it up, then gasps when he sees what's inside.

"Oh, Daddy," he says as he carefully removes the new collar.

It's finer than his regular collar he wears at home and at work but sturdier than the choker he currently has on. The many, *many* diamonds sparkle in the sunlight, and his eyes well up with tears as he slowly turns it this way and that.

"Why don't you read the inscription," I say, nodding towards the heart-shaped tag.

Yes, I know I'm cheesy. No, I don't care.

He bites his lip and turns over the disk in his fingers. "Daddy and kitten forever," he says thickly. "Oh."

He frowns, and I'm not quite sure he gets it yet, but that's okay because there's a second part to this gift.

"Here," I say, handing him the small box. "This is for you as well."

He swallows as he carefully places the new collar down on the bag it came out of, then opens the lid of the box.

His eyes don't just fill this time. The tears spill down his face.

"Oh, *Daddy,*" he whispers.

My chest is tight, and my eyes are also wet as I take the box from him and ease out the ring that's diamond-encrusted to match the collar. I take his hand and place the ring on the tip of his left finger, pausing to look into his gorgeous brown eyes.

"My darling Charlie," I say as steadily as I can. "Will you marry me? Will you wear my ring and my collar for the rest of our lives together? Will you promise to always be my beautiful kitten?"

A sob makes his chest shudder, and his face is blotchy, but he shakes his head so vigorously as he gasps for air. *"Yes, Daddy!"* he cries, practically shoving his finger through the hole and proudly showing me that the ring fits. Then he throws his arms around me and lets out another loud sob. "Yes, Daddy, yes! Oh my god. I love you so much. I can't believe this is happening."

I laugh as relief courses through me. I really hoped he'd say yes. I can't imagine my life without my sweet baby boy. But in the moment, I really wasn't sure what was going to happen, so I understand where my kitten is coming from.

"Oh, Charlie," I say as I hug him tightly and place smackers all over his face, finally capturing his lips for a long, passionate kiss. "I love you so much, too. You're my everything. I want to spend every day of the rest of my life loving you. You make me so happy."

He takes a shuddery breath, then leans back so he's looking in my eyes. "You found me when I was a stray, but then you gave me a home. You collared me and loved me until I was no longer feral. You'll always have my heart, Daddy. Forever."

"Forever is all I ask," I tell him.

THANK you so much for reading Miller and Charlie's story! If you enjoyed it, please leave a review so that others can discover their book.

If you want more contemporary fairy tale retellings with Daddies, keep reading to discover **Three** (The Three Little Pigs), **Golden** (Goldilocks and the Three Bears), and **Wild Ride** (Little Red Riding Hood). For my other fairy tales, check out the **three-book box set** of Cinderella, Beauty and the Beast, and Rapunzel!

If you'd like to discover my contemporary American pen name, HJ Welch, please take a look at the **Pine Cove** complete box set, available in eBook and audio!

IF YOU'D LIKE to be the first to know what fairy tale I'll be working on next, make sure to join my Facebook group, **Helen's Jewels**. We also have a lot of fun with games and giveaways, as well as ARC opportunities.

THANK YOU TO MY TEAM!

Cover Design: Cate Ashwood

Editing: Meg Cooper

Proof Reading: Tanja Ongkiehong

General awesomeness: Ed Davies, AK Faulkner, my hubby, and our cats.

THREE

All good things come in threes...

When three shy best friends sign up to a dating app to finally lose their virginity by the end of the year, they don't expect to all fall for the same gorgeous, slightly scary-looking Daddy. The only solution? Let him choose who he wants to bed. Except he doesn't...

Jacob didn't become a billionaire before hitting thirty-five by making compromises. What he wants, he *gets*. So why should he choose between these adorable boys when he can devour all three? Instead, he tells them to decide on an order, and then he'll spoil each of them one after the other in a way they'll never forget.

Will one night each be enough? And can that really be all they need to fall in love? One thing's for sure, when danger comes calling, this Daddy will discover just how far he'll go to protect his three little piggies.

Three is a super steamy, standalone MMMM gay romance novel featuring a Daddy wolf ready to huff and puff his way into three hearts, best friends who discover something more between them, a box full of abandoned kittens, and a guaranteed HEA with absolutely no cliffhanger.

Click here to get the Three eBook

GOLDEN

Can three very hungry bears find their own sweet golden boy?

GOLDIE

Thanks to my no-good ex, I'm up to my eyeballs in debt…to an adult entertainment company. The owner offers me the chance of a lifetime: if I keep my lips zipped about why I'm there, I can work off the loan in front of the camera. I'm thrilled, but self-conscious: who wants to work with a skinny twink like me? Then the biggest, scariest star of all asks for me. In fact, Daddy *demands* me. And, like both his partners warn me: what Daddy wants, Daddy gets. Can I really handle three bears? As they close in on me, I realise…it's too late to run.

DADDY

Goldie is shy, innocent, brand-new…and totally irresistible. I'm going to make him ours. The three of us have enough love for a fourth. It's supposed to be only for a weekend, but our golden angel's secrets betray a broken soul that needs mending…and I'm the man to do it. Goldie's sleazy ex is too cold for him, and this weekend might be too hot. But the four of us together? That feels just right. And when I find out why Goldie's really there, we'll stop at nothing to save our golden boy.

Golden is a super steamy, standalone MMMM gay romance novella featuring a picturesque cottage in the English countryside, lashings of praise for a shy boy, one very fat cat who knows best, enough porridge for four hungry tummies, and a guaranteed HEA with absolutely no cliffhanger.

Click here to get the Golden eBook

WILD RIDE

A sexy surprise is waiting in the woods...

RED

Chased into the forest in the middle of the night, my only hope of survival is the man I used to obsess over. Now I'm all grown up, I won't miss this opportunity to thank him. Our chemistry is immediate and off the charts, and I'm not looking for a Forever Daddy. My Very First Daddy is all I need. But when he surprises me with a present that awakens something new in me, I know I can't quit.

HUNTER

I've never been anyone's Daddy before, but Red needs me in a way that melts my grizzly heart. I'll do anything for him. But if my recent, brutal divorce has taught me anything, it's that I'm not much of a catch. Does a beautiful young thing like Red really want me? His brother might be my best friend, but his father hates us both and will do all he can to keep us apart. When trouble comes knocking on my door, though, I know I'll do anything to save this boy I've fallen for.

***Wild Ride** is a super steamy, standalone MM gay romance novella featuring a boy who discovers a love of lingerie, a sassy grandma, a loyal pooch the size of a wolf, something scary lurking in the woods, and a guaranteed HEA with absolutely no cliffhanger.*

Click here to get the Wild Ride eBook

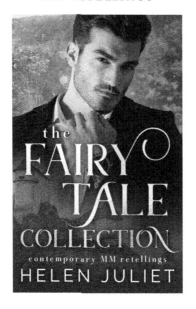

very protective and caring. When danger comes knocking on their door, will Joshua and Darius's blossoming love be strong enough to save each other?

A Right Royal Affair

Nobody knows that Prince James of the United Kingdom is bisexual, and as he's sixth in line to the throne, it needs to stay that way. But when he meets the cheeky, outrageously gay Essex boy, Theo Glass, everything could change. Against his better judgement, James asks Theo to help him put on a royal charity ball to remember. Can they resist their mutual attraction for a whole week alone in a picturesque castle, or will true love bloom?

Hair Out of Place

Raphael d'Oro is a secret prince who has spent his entire life exiled in a London penthouse. But now he's in a race against time to get back to his tiny European nation to claim the throne that's rightfully his and save his people. Good thing he has his insanely hot older bodyguard to take care of him. But Griff Thompson would never want someone as inexperienced as Raphie, would he? Even *if* they keep finding themselves in places with only one bed…

Click here for the Fairy Tale Collection eBook

Click here for the Fairy Tale Collection audio

Bodyguard Scout Duffy doesn't know what's worse: the fact that his scorching one-night-stand, Emery Klein, is his bratty new client, or the fact that he doesn't even remember Scout. But Emery's life is in danger thanks to his out and proud charity work, and once he finally recognizes Scout, their chemistry in undeniable.

-

Homeward Bound

Swift Coal just found out he's a father, and his daughter (and her cranky cat) are coming to stay. His best friend's younger brother, Micha Perkins, has nowhere to go and a wrongfully tattered reputation. He's relieved when Swift asks him to be a live-in babysitter. He just has to hide his lifelong crush. Easy, because Swift is straight—right?

-

Bright Horizon

With sixteen years between them, baker Ben Turner and lawyer Elias Solomon have no idea their crush is mutual. But when Ben inherits his long-lost family's estate and becomes an overnight millionaire, Elias swears to protect the innocent younger man from the vultures circling him. To unravel the mystery of the inheritance, they must go to England to confront Ben's estranged relatives…and their feelings for each other.

-

Crossed Paths

Raj Bhat is done living in the shadows. It's time for him to take charge of his own destiny and tell the man he's fallen for how he really feels.

-

Midnight Sky

It's the night before New Year's Eve. Taylan Demir is all alone, and he's just lost his dog. Except when his handsome customer, Hudson Perkins, comes to his rescue, Taylan doesn't just get his dog back. He's suddenly got a hot date, and maybe someone to kiss when the clock strikes midnight.

-

Memory Lane

Angel Shields saved Jay Coal's life in high school, and Jay has secretly loved his straight best friend ever since. Now Angel's back in town with amnesia after a suspicious work accident and it's Jay's turn to rescue him. He pretends to be Angel's fiancé to see him in the hospital, but with his scrambled-up memory, Angel's not sure it's fictional after all. He just knows he loves Jay more than ever.

-

Thin Ice

Kamran's ex broke his heart, tricked him into aiding a bank robbery, and now he wants him to do one last job. There's only one way to say no: seek the protective custody of the biggest, grumpiest FBI agent ever, Lee Marshall. And pretend to be his boyfriend for a week-long family reunion in their giant mansion. Wait, what?

-

Calm Shores

Gorgeous, sophisticated Dante walks into Oliver's bar and orders…a boyfriend?! Dante needs a man to keep his mother from setting him back up with his awful, cheating ex, and Oliver is up for the challenge.

-

Fresh Snow

Emery Klein is throwing the best Christmas party ever, but his fiancé, Scout Duffy, and all their friends have something more exciting in mind.

-

Each Pine Cove book can be read as a stand alone and has its own happy ever after. But if you read the whole series, you'll see a lot of familiar faces!

Click here to get the Pine Cove eBook bundle

Click here to get the Pine Cove audio bundle

ABOUT THE AUTHOR

Helen Juliet is a contemporary MM romance author living in London with her husband and two balls of fluff that occasionally pretend to be cats. She began writing at an early age, later honing her craft online in the world of fanfiction on sites like Wattpad. Fifteen years and over half a million words later, she sought out original MM novels to read. By the end of 2016 she had written her first book of her own, and in 2017 she achieved her lifelong dream of becoming a fulltime author.

Helen also writes contemporary American MM romance as HJ Welch.

You can contact Helen Juliet via social media:
Newsletter (with FREE original stories) – https://www. subscribepage.com/helenjuliet
Website – www.helenjuliet.com
Facebook Group – Helen's Jewels
Facebook Page – @helenjulietauthor
Instagram – @helenjwrites
Twitter – @helenjwrites

.

Printed in Great Britain
by Amazon